The Vampire's Kiss

RAMONA GRAY

Adult Reading Material

Published by:
EK Publishing Inc.

Cover art by:
The Final Wrap

ISBN: 978-1-926483-31-3

Chapter One

Abigail Winters had no idea what was happening. One minute she was hurrying home from her mundane job as a coffee barista in the worse thunderstorm she had ever seen. The next, she was lying flat on her back in the middle of a forest with the rain falling on her face.

She sat up, rubbing the knot that was forming on the back of her head, and peered around curiously. She was sure she had seen a bright orb of light hovering to the left of her before everything went black. She looked around for her purse, wanting to grab her cell phone and call someone. Who she wasn't sure – the police maybe.

Her purse was nowhere to be seen and she sighed and stood cautiously, waiting to see if she was going to pass out. Her head was aching and her new jeans, the ones she was so proud to buy because they were a size smaller than her last pair, were shredded at the knees and covered in mud.

Was she dead? Didn't people say there was a white light when you died? She looked around as the rain continued to fall. It was dark and scary and if this was heaven, she would hate to see what hell looked like.

She moved forward slowly, squinting in the dark and watching her feet so she didn't trip over the exposed roots of the trees around her.

She was frightened, but not panicking. At least, not yet. There was a part of her, a very large part, which was convinced she was dreaming. Any moment now she would wake up in her bed with the sheets tangled around her legs and her alarm clock shrieking at her.

She took a deep breath. The air smelled sweet and clean, nothing like the smog of the city, and she wondered vaguely if someone had kidnapped her and dumped her in the country.

Don't be ridiculous, Abby. Who would kidnap you? You're a nobody.

All perfectly true. She wasn't an heiress with a million-dollar inheritance, she wasn't a famous singer or movie star. Truth be told she had less than twenty dollars in her bank account at the moment. She was just plain, fat Abby. Always had been, always would be.

Yes, but don't forget that you're fat Abby with fifteen pounds less fat.

Also true. She ran her hands down her size eighteen jeans. She was thrilled when she went down a size in pants. She carried most of her weight in her ass and her hips, and to be down a pants size meant that her healthy eating and exercising was working. She hated exercising but she was becoming addicted to the results.

Um, Abby? Not to rain on your parade but in case you've forgotten, you're either dead or something very, very weird is going on. Maybe celebrate your weight loss victory another time, what do you say?

Very good advice. If she wasn't dead then she needed to find the nearest phone and call the police.

She stumbled through the trees. She had no idea if she was moving deeper into the woods or not but she couldn't just stand there. She had to keep moving.

"She looks like a lost lamb. Does she not, Toron?"

Abby shrieked and whipped around. Two men were standing behind her. They were dressed similarly in faded green pants and white shirts. One was tall and dark and the other short and blond.

"Aye, she does, Alex," the blond man said gravely.

"Are you lost little lamb? Lost in the woods?" The one named Toron crooned.

Abby backed up a step. There was something about the two men that was making all the hair on her body attempt to stand up. Adrenaline was flooding through her veins and her limbs trembled in response.

She stumbled back another step as the men moved closer. Alex inhaled deeply. "I can smell her fear. It smells delicious."

Toron grinned at him. "I'm feeling generous this evening. Why don't you have the first drink?"

"Don't mind if I do," Alex said cheerfully. He was standing in front of her and pushing her against a tree before Abby had realized he'd moved.

Her head banged on the tree, the knot screaming in protest, and she screamed shrilly into the cold night air.

"Oh yes, little lamb – go ahead and scream. There's no one to hear you and I do love it when the lambs scream," Alex whispered.

He was holding her with one hand across the top of her chest and she grabbed his arm and tried to yank it away from her. His arm was hard as iron. She struggled futilely, unable to believe that the small man could hold her so easily with just one hand. She stared at his pale skin, her eyes dark and wide with panic, and he giggled like a demented child.

"You're a big one but I don't mind. More of you to drink, right?"

She slapped him across the face as hard as she could. His head rocked back but his hand never moved from her chest.

He hissed at her and she screamed as fresh adrenaline poured into her veins. Alex was grinning at her and exposing his long, white fangs.

"You don't ever want to hit me, little lamb. Not that it matters – you'll be dead in a few minutes."

"Oh, get on with it, would you, Alex. I want my turn. You shouldn't play with your food anyway. Didn't your mother ever tell - "

Toron suddenly arched his back as a startled look crossed his face. "Alex - "

Abby sucked in her breath when Toron suddenly exploded in a shower of ash and blood. Alex screamed, a sound of rage and fear, at the man standing in the trees. He held a long, curved blade in one hand and he smiled bitterly at Alex.

"You would kill your own kind!" Alex screamed again and, forgetting Abby entirely, he lunged for the stranger. His fingernails were lengthening, becoming long and wickedly sharp talons, and he moved so quickly that he was nothing but a blur.

Alex was quick but the stranger was faster. The blade plunged through Alex's chest and his scream of fury became a long, gurgling moan. Abby sunk to the ground, wrapping her arms around her knees as the stranger yanked the blade free and wiped it on Alex's shirt. He stepped back as Alex exploded.

Abby watched disinterestedly as the man approached her, sheathing his blade into the holder at his waist. He crouched in front of her and took her chin in his hand, tilting her head first one way and then the other as he examined her neck.

He was tall and broad with long dark hair tied back in a neat ponytail. His eyes were a silvery grey and his skin was pale and smooth. He had a broad nose and high cheekbones, and his jaw was covered in dark stubble.

"Are you going to kill me?" Abby asked dully.

He shook his head. "No. Get up, girl."

He heaved her to her feet with one hard hand under her arm and gave her a look of disgust when she swayed. He eyed her up and down and another grimace of disgust passed across his face.

She would have been offended if she hadn't noticed his teeth. They were very white and, despite the rain and the darkness, she had no problem seeing his fangs. She moaned and he shook his head impatiently.

"I said I wouldn't hurt you. Come on, girl." He dragged her through the trees, moving so quickly that she was soon out of breath and struggling to catch up.

He grunted with frustration and slowed down a fraction, his hand tightening on her wrist when she tried to pull free.

"Please let go of me," she panted.

"So you can run? You'll be dead before morning if I do," he snapped.

"Where are we going?"

"I'm taking you to your own kind. Now keep your mouth shut and hurry up."

In less than fifteen minutes they were at the edge of the forest. He stopped, his eyes roaming the large field in front of them. She stood next to him, panting and trying to control her runaway heartbeat as he rolled his eyes.

"Have you considered eating less and moving more, human?"

"Fuck you," she puffed.

He laughed. "The lamb shows spirit."

She glared at him and he suddenly cupped her face and pulled her forward until her face was only inches from his. He grinned at her, his fangs looking very long and very sharp, and she swallowed nervously.

"Although I do enjoy fucking a human, you're not my type." He let his gaze travel down her body and back up to her face. "A little too big for my tastes. Still, you are rather attractive – perhaps I could make an exception."

She flushed bright red and yanked her head from his grip. He returned his gaze to the field. "We're going to be moving very quickly across the field. Keep up. You'll regret it if you don't. Do you understand me?"

He stared into her dark brown eyes. His eyes were grey and cold and she nodded, although she was almost positive that she would not be able to keep up with him. She wasn't going to tell him that. He would probably kill her rather than give her the chance to try.

"Good. Let's - "

He stopped, his head cocked to the side, and his eyebrows drew down in a frown.

"What - "

"Shut up!" He hissed.

She closed her mouth with a snap as he dropped her wrist. She took a few steps backward, wondering if she could sneak away without him noticing. Before she could dart into the trees, a silver mesh dropped onto the man in front of her.

He hissed in agony as he collapsed to the ground. She watched in horror as his skin began to smoke. She reached for the net but two men and a woman dropped from the skies above her and blocked her from grabbing it.

"Hello human." The woman smiled at her, revealing her own set of fangs, and Abby moaned with terror.

Chapter Two

"Why would you be dragging a human through the woods instead of drinking from her?" The woman stared at the man who had rescued her.

From her spot on the ground, Abby watched as the woman traced her long fingernail across the stranger's face. Wearing gloves, the three vampires had chained him to a tree with long silver chains before removing the mesh. Abby had winced at the marks on his skin that the mesh had left. The woman had ripped off his shirt, revealing a pale muscular torso. The silver chains were slowly sinking into his skin and she wondered if after a few hours they would simply rip his body apart. Smoke was rising steadily from his body and he had to be in incredible pain, but his face was serene and his grey eyes revealed nothing.

The woman glanced at Abby before looking back at the chained man. "Do you keep her as your pet? Feed from her when you need to?"

He refused to answer and she swiped across his face with her long nails. They dug long, bloody furrows into his face, and Abby winced but the vampire didn't flinch.

"You wouldn't mind if we have a taste of your pet, would you?" The vampire standing above her grinned and yanked her to her feet. He cupped the back of her neck and stared at her. His eyes were a very light blue, and Abby could see herself reflected back in them.

"That's right, look at me, sweet one," he whispered. She could feel a strange, heavy warmth coursing through her body and she smiled a little. For the first time since she had woken on the floor of the forest, she wasn't afraid.

The vampire smiled again and stroked her cheek with his thumb. "You're very pretty. Did you know that?"

She gave him a dreamy, lost look. "Thank you."

"Lift your head, my pretty. Let me see that beautiful throat."

Still staring into his eyes, she lifted her head obediently. He dipped his head and nuzzled her throat. She gasped. Her nipples were hard little pebbles in her bra and there was sudden wetness between her thighs.

"Shall I taste you?" He murmured.

"Yes, oh yes please," she whimpered.

He opened his mouth, his fangs lengthening, and she let her head fall back until she was staring at the night sky. The clouds were parting and she could see the moon shining brightly. Her entire body shivered and she waited breathlessly for his bite.

Before he could plunge his fangs into the

throbbing vein in her neck, there was a sharp whistle. He dropped her and she fell bonelessly to the ground, panting and moaning as desire coursed through her body.

The whistle came again, sharp and piercing, and then the vampire above her made a soft grunt. He looked down to see the dagger sticking out of his chest and reached for it with pale hands. Before he could pull it from his chest his entire body exploded, splattering blood and ash over Abby.

The female vampire screamed angrily as the second male vampire turned and stared into the trees. A bear of a man stepped out and drove a sword through his chest. He yanked the sword free, stepping back as a glut of blood sprayed from the vampire's chest. The female screamed again as the vampire exploded and then she was standing next to the man, her hand wrapping around his throat. Despite his size, she lifted him easily and threw him against the tree. He slammed into it, his head bouncing off the tree, and fell to the ground. She pounced on him and leaned over, grabbing his hair with one pale hand and yanking his head back to bare his throat.

Before she could sink her teeth into him, a second woman, pale and blonde, stepped out of the trees and tapped her gently on the back. The vampire whirled and hissed as the woman, her hand a blur, slashed her across the throat with a short blade. The vampire's head slid from her body and landed with a soft thump at the woman's feet. She walked away as the body turned to ash.

"Neil, are you okay?" She asked as she walked

towards Abby. Her voice was low and musical and Abby didn't need to see her mouth to know that she was a vampire. It was in the way she moved, in the easy grace that flowed through her body.

She held out her hand and, after a second, Abby took it. The woman pulled her to her feet and smiled at her. "What's your name?"

"Abigail...Abby," Abby stuttered as Neil stood and hurried toward the man still chained to the tree.

She noticed with a curious type of numbness that he wore no gloves as he unwrapped the silver chains that bound the man to the tree.

Human, she decided, as the vampire standing in front of her looked her up and down. "I do not think she is from here."

Neil caught the vampire as he crumpled forward and he heaved him over his shoulder. "Christ, Val. You're goddamn heavy."

Val grunted with pain. "I can walk."

Neil shook his head. "No, you can't. I can smell your flesh from here." He made a grimace of disgust and shifted Val on his shoulder. "Eone, we need to get back to the house. Right now."

"I know." Eone stared at Abby. "Do we bring her with us?"

Val shook his head. "No, she's too slow. It's why they caught us in the first place."

"We're not leaving her," Neil replied. "She'll die if we do."

"I do not think she is from here," Eone repeated herself.

Val lifted his head weakly and stared at the two women. "She isn't. I saw the light that brought her here."

Abby took a deep breath. "Please, can someone tell me what's going on? Where am I? Who are you?"

Eone smiled at her and Abby felt warmth surging through her pelvis again. She shook her head and made herself look away from Eone's gaze.

"Come, pretty one." Eone took her hand. "We'll explain everything when we are safe."

৵ ৵

"Jesus Christ! What the fuck happened?" A short man, his grey hair thin and stretched across the top of his head in a vain attempt to hide his bald spot, watched as Neil dumped Val on the couch.

"What do you think happened, Bert?" Neil said. "Leeches."

He glanced at Eone and Val. "No offense."

"Who is this?" A short, plump woman, her dark hair pulled into a bun on top of her head, stared curiously at Abby.

"This is Abby." Eone tugged her forward and stroked her hair. She had plaited it this morning but it was starting to come loose from the braid.

More people were crowding into the room, men and women of varying ages and sizes, and Abby shrank back as they gathered around her.

"Don't be afraid, sweet one," Eone smiled at her. "We will not harm you."

"Please tell me what's happening," Abby whispered.

Bert stared at her. "Christ, she's another transplant. Who wants to try and explain it this time?"

The woman with the bun stepped forward. "I will." She took Abby's hand and led her to a second couch across from the one that Val was lying on.

"My name is Maria. It's nice to meet you, Abby."

"It's nice to meet you too. Are you – are you a vampire?" Abby stared at her.

Maria shook her head. "No I'm not. I'm human like you. Only Eone and Val are vampires."

She took Abby's cold hand in her warm ones. "Abby, do you remember what happened to you?"

"I was – was walking home from work. It was raining and dark and then there was this weird glowing orb. The next thing I remember was waking up in the forest."

Maria sighed. "All of this is going to be hard for you to believe but I need you to try and have an open mind. Can you do that, Abby?"

"Yes."

"Good. That glowing orb was a – a doorway of sorts. It sucked you from your world and into ours."

Abby frowned. "Am I on an alien planet?"

Maria shook her head. "Not exactly. It's what you call earth – only a different version of it."

She glanced behind her at a tall, thin man and he smiled encouragingly at her. "Our version has not only humans but other creatures as well. Vampires like Eone and Abby and other different species."

"Like what?" Abby rubbed the knot at the back of her head.

"We'll explain more later. Right now, I want to make sure you understand that you are no longer on your earth. There are many things in this world that will seek to harm you, and you must stay with us for your own protection. Do you understand that? None of us will hurt you."

Abby's eyes slid to Val and Eone and Maria grasped her chin and turned her face towards her. "Eone and Val will not harm you."

"They're good vampires?"

Bert snorted and Maria glared at him. "Yes, Abby. They're good vampires. Most vampires prey on humans, seek them out to feed on and turn, or keep them as pets. However, there are some who have joined forces with the humans. They wish to create a world of peace like we do. Val and Eone are two of those vampires."

"How do I get back to my own world?"

Maria gave her a look of sympathy. "You cannot, Abby. I'm sorry but there is no way to return to the life you once led."

Abby stared at her in shock. "But – but you said the orb was a doorway. I just need to find another one and –"

Maria squeezed her hands. "There is no guarantee that the orb would return you to your own world. Most likely you would be sent to yet another world. There are many different worlds."

Abby could feel the tears sliding down her cheeks as Maria squeezed her hands again. "I'm sorry, Abby. Why don't you come with me? You can bathe and I'll find you some clean clothes, and then you can lie down for a bit. Things will be clearer once you've gotten some rest."

Abby stood and allowed the smaller woman to lead her from the room.

ॐ ⳬ

"Do you feel better, Abby?" Maria smiled at her when Abby entered the kitchen.

"A little. How long have I been sleeping?" She pulled nervously at the top and pants that Maria had given her. The pants were too big, she suspected Maria nicked them from one of the men, and the top too small. It clung tightly to her large breasts.

"Only a few hours. Here, have some tea."

Abby accepted the cup and sipped at the steaming liquid. It had a woodsy, velvety taste to it and she stared curiously at it. "What type of tea is this?"

Maria smiled. "None that you would recognize."

"Are you from my world?" Abby asked tentatively.

"No. But I was married to one who was," Maria replied. "At least I think you're from the same world. You speak in a similar manner to him. Tell me – do you have metal wagons that propel themselves using a liquid that catches fire? Metal tubes that fly in the sky?"

Abby nodded. "Yes."

Maria smiled. "I thought so."

"Where is your husband?"

"He's dead," Maria replied bluntly.

"I – I'm sorry."

"It was a long time ago. Are you hungry?

Would you - "

There was shouting from the living room and Abby followed Maria as she hurried out of the kitchen.

"I ain't letting him bite me." A redheaded woman was staring furiously at Neil. "You have no right to ask me to do that, you big lug! You think I don't know what will happen afterwards? I won't become his meal ticket every night just because he knows I won't be able to stop myself."

"Erin, if we don't do something he's going to die," Neil said desperately.

"So, let him die! What do I care if some dirty leech lives or dies?" Erin shouted.

"That leech has saved our lives more times than we can count," Neil said through gritted teeth. "Are you honestly okay with letting him die?"

Erin didn't reply and he stared around the room at the other women. "Is there not one of you who will help him?"

"What's going on?" Abby whispered to Maria as Neil went and knelt beside the couch that Val was lying on. The vampire was noticeably paler, and his wounds from the mesh and the chain were still oozing a steady flow of blood.

"Val needs human blood to heal. He's going to die if he doesn't get it," Maria replied. Her hands were wringing together and she was staring anxiously at Eone.

"Eone, what if one of the women was to slice her arm and drain some blood. Val can drink it that way. It will heal him."

Eone shook her head. "It will help but not

quickly enough. You know how this works, Maria. A human's blood works best when we can drink directly from the source. We do not have time to drain blood and wait for it to heal him. By tomorrow night vampires will be all over this place. We killed three - "

"Five," Val said weakly from the couch.

She rolled her eyes. "We killed five of them tonight. They will belong to a large nest. We are too far west for them to be striking out on their own. The others in their nest will search for them tomorrow night when they don't return. They will find the house easily."

"This is all your fault!" Erin suddenly hissed at Abby. "Val and the others should have let you die. You're going to get us all killed!"

"Erin, enough!" Maria said sharply. She turned to Abby. "Ignore her. She's just frightened."

"Why does it have to be a woman?" Abby asked quietly. "Can't one of the men do it?"

Eone laughed, a tinkling soft sound that made the hair on Abby's arms stand up. "The act of taking blood from a human is a very sensual experience, Abby. Once a vampire has fed from a human, there is a connection between them that humans cannot resist."

She drifted closer and stroked Abby's soft hair. "Sometimes the act of feeding even leads to the act of lovemaking. We vampires are very aware of the needs of our humans. We are attentive and thorough lovers, Abby."

Abby stared into Eone's dark blue eyes. An ache was starting up in her pelvis and she wondered what it would be like to press her mouth against Eone's. Wondered how it would feel to have Eone's soft hand squeezing her breast, her thumb rubbing against her nipple as Abby lifted her neck and let the vampire drink from her.

"Would you like that, Abby? Would you like to feel my touch? I could make you feel so good if you'll let me." Eone's fangs lengthened. "The human males are not willing to feel such a connection, a desire, for a male vampire so they will not help Val. I, however, have no issue with pleasing a female human."

"Eone!" Neil's voice broke through the fog that had drifted into Abby's head and she took a step back as Eone tore her gaze from hers.

"What?" She asked petulantly.

"In case you've forgotten – Val is dying." Neil glared at her.

Eone sighed. "I have not forgotten. But I am thirsty."

"Knock it off, Eone," Neil snarled. He turned back to the people grouped loosely together. "Please, someone needs to help him."

"Forget it, Neil," Val said hoarsely. "They will never agree to it. They only let Eone and me stay because deep down they're afraid of us." He raised his head and bared his fangs at them. "And they should be."

"Val! You're not helping," Neil moaned. "Please. He has done so much for us. Can not one of you - "

"I'll do it."

Her voice, low and husky, could barely be

heard.

Neil swivelled and stared at Abby. "What?"

"I said I would do it."

"Abby, honey, you're tired and confused and you don't quite understand what this means. If you let him feed from you, there will be an obsession that you will not be able to control." Maria squeezed her arm. "You will yearn for him in ways that I cannot even begin to explain. You will need to leave our group until the obsession fades or risk going mad."

She hesitated and glanced at Val. "Unless Val continues to feed from you until we can find a safe place for you to – "

"I will not," Val interrupted darkly.

"You asshole!" Neil growled at him. "She is your only chance."

Maria squeezed her arm again. "You don't want to do this, Abby."

"He saved my life in the forest," Abby said. "I owe him a debt."

She stared distastefully at Val. "Besides, I've never obsessed over a man in my life and I'm certainly not going to start with him. I'll be fine."

"Thank you, Abby," Neil said gratefully.

Maria frowned at him. "We cannot let her do this, Neil. She doesn't understand - "

"Quiet, Maria! She's made her choice," Neil spat.

He grabbed Val and hauled him into a sitting position. "You just got lucky, Val."

Val frowned as blood dripped down his face. "I do not want to feed from her. She will taste bad.

The big ones always do."

Abby flushed a brilliant red and Neil slapped Val viciously across the face.

"Shut your fucking face, Val! This woman is about to save your life and you'll be grateful for it."

He put his arm around Val and hauled him to his feet. He turned to Abigail. "Follow me."

❧ ❧

Abigail watched nervously as Neil helped Val lay down on the bed. He turned on the lantern beside the bed and the room was illuminated with a dim light. He smiled at Abigail and patted the bed beside Val.

"Lie down, Abby."

She moved nervously across the room and lay down beside Val's body. He stared at her as Neil patted her arm awkwardly. "Thank you for doing this. He's being an ungrateful bastard but trust me, he is actually grateful."

Abby nodded and felt a thin thread of fear when Neil headed towards the door. "Are you not staying?"

Neil shook his head. "No. Try and relax, okay? It will make it easier."

He left the room and closed the door behind him.

❧ ❧

Val rose up on his elbow, wincing as the wounds dripped fresh blood, and stared down at the clearly frightened woman. He didn't want to feed from her. He would have no way to avoid her and it would be weeks before her need for him wore off. If she didn't go mad first. He had no wish to have the human pining after him, begging him to feed from her again or have sex with her. Some vampires enjoyed the way humans obsessed after them but he did not. He preferred to feed, fuck the human if it was a female, and then leave.

He sighed. He had no choice. He was growing weaker by the hour and Neil was right – the wounds from the silver would kill him if he didn't feed. He thought briefly of making it easier for her, of using his powers to seduce and calm her, but dismissed it almost immediately. Sometimes a human's need would be less if the feeding was frightening and painful. It wouldn't kill her desire for him entirely, but it might give him a moment or two of peace from her in the following weeks.

"Should I – do I do anything special?" She whispered.

He continued to stare at her. She really was rather attractive, he thought wearily. Her dark brown eyes were framed with long, thick lashes and her skin was pale and blemish free. His gaze dropped to her mouth. Her full pink lips were trembling and there was a strand of her dark hair caught against them. He brushed it away, rolling his eyes when she flinched.

"Take off your shirt," he grunted.

She hesitated and he gave her an impatient look. "Do you want blood on it?"

She shook her head and quickly took it off. She lay back on the bed and gave him another nervous look. Despite the fact that her breasts were covered by her bra, she kept her arms crossed over them.

"Lift your head."

She swallowed audibly and lifted her head, turning her face away and closing her eyes. He stared at her throat. Her fear was making her pulse pound and he could see it at the base of her throat. Her blood was calling to him and, without warning, he dipped his head and plunged his fangs deep into her throbbing vein. She cried out with pain and fear and he clamped his arm down across her thick waist, pinning her to the bed as she tried to struggle free.

Her blood filled his mouth, warm and rich and tasting sweeter than any blood he'd ever tasted before. He groaned as his cock hardened in his pants and he pulled her closer. He drank and drank as her struggles weakened and she relaxed against the bed. He couldn't get enough of her and as he swallowed her warm blood, feeling his wounds heal and his strength come back, he tugged her arms away from her breasts and wormed his fingers under her bra. He cupped her naked breast. It was warm and full and he squeezed it gently, rubbing his thumb across her nipple. It hardened immediately and she moaned - a sound full of longing and need that made his cock throb in response.

He pushed his thigh between her legs, pressing it against her pussy and she squeezed his thigh with hers, rubbing her crotch against his leg like a cat in heat. He continued to drink long after his wounds had healed, as he cupped and caressed her firm breast.

He could feel her pulse weakening and she stopped squeezing his thigh and let her legs fall apart limply. With a harsh gasp he pulled his mouth free from her throat and moved his hand from her breast. Panting loudly, he stared down at the woman. He had taken so much of her blood that she had fainted. He stared at the holes in her neck, licking her blood from his lips while his entire body screamed at him to continue.

With a loud grunt, he jumped off the bed and backed away. Jesus, he hadn't lost control like that in centuries. Even from across the room her blood still called to him and, before he could give in to his urge and drain her completely, he turned and fled the room.

Chapter Three

Abigail groaned and opened her eyes. She stared at the blue sky above her as her bed swayed gently. She could hear the snorting of horses and the low murmur of voices. She closed her eyes. She was so tired and she didn't understand what was happening. Where was she?

"Abby?" A woman's soft voice forced her heavy lids up again and she stared blearily at the dark-haired woman.

"Maria." It all came back to her in a rush of remembrance and she sighed as tears slipped down her cheeks. She was in hell.

"Don't cry, Abby." Maria's voice sounded worried and she smoothed the hair back from Abby's brow. "You're okay, my love. Don't cry now."

She opened her eyes and stared at Maria. "I'm not dreaming."

"No, honey. You're not. I'm sorry."

"Why am I so tired?" She wanted to sit up but lacked the strength.

"Val took too much from you. You'll feel better once you have something to eat and rest more."

"What time is it?"

"It's early morning. Can you sit up, Abby? You need to drink some tea. It will help restore your strength."

With Maria's help, Abby sat up. She looked around wearily. She was in a wagon being driven by Neil. The rest of the group was walking, and talking amongst themselves.

"Where are we going?"

"We need to keep moving. We're deep in their territory, and it's best if we get to the outskirts as quickly as possible." Maria held a cup to her mouth. "Drink this."

Abby drank the thick, dark liquid. It tasted spicy and warm and she gulped it down eagerly.

Maria smiled at her. "That's my good girl. Here, try eating this." She handed Abby a piece of dried meat.

Abby stared at it curiously. "What kind of meat is this?"

"Nothing you'll know. Eat it, Abby. It's rich with nutrients."

Abby bit into the meat and chewed gingerly. It was tough but good, and she ate three pieces and drank another cup of tea before Maria helped her to lie back in the blankets.

"Go to sleep, Abby. You're safe with us." Maria stroked her forehead and Abigail closed her eyes and slept.

When she woke for a second time, the sun was nearly setting and the wagon was pulling to a stop in front of a large house. The place looked deserted and she sat up. She was feeling less tired and more like herself.

"Where are we?"

Maria turned from where she was sitting beside Neil. "An abandoned house. We're going to stay here for the night."

She hopped down from the wagon and Abby squirmed past the supplies that were packed around her. She climbed out of the wagon, smiling gratefully at the young man who rushed forward and steadied her when she staggered and nearly fell.

"Thank you."

He smiled at her. "You're welcome."

"I'm Abigail."

"David."

"It's nice to meet you, David."

"You as well."

Neil jumped out of the wagon and glanced at the setting sun before looking at the bottom of the wagon. Abby followed his gaze and frowned a little. She hadn't seen many wagons but this one looked strange to her. There was a long wooden compartment attached to the bottom of it and one side of it was on hinges.

"What is that?"

"It's where Eone and Val sleep their daysleep." Neil cleared his throat as Abigail paled and backed away from the wagon.

"I don't want him to touch me again," she whispered. She started to tremble, remembering the fear and the pain as he had bitten into her.

It didn't hurt for long. You remember how good

it felt when he touched your breast. You wanted him to fuck you, you know you did.

Maria gave Neil a confused look. "Why is she afraid?"

The door to the compartment started to open and Abigail backed up until she bumped into David.

Neil put his large hand on the door, holding it shut for a moment.

"She should go in the house," he said nervously, staring at Abby.

David held out his hand. "Here, Abby, let me help you into the house." She took his hand and he led her up the stairs of the porch and into the house.

Neil waited until she had disappeared into the house and then lifted the side of the compartment. Eone slid out, followed by Val, and she stretched prettily before looking around curiously. "God, I'm so hungry. I don't suppose we're near a village?"

Neil shook his head and she sighed. "Ugh, deer again."

Val's nose wrinkled and he leaned against the wagon. Eone looked back at him. "Are you coming?"

He shook his head. "No."

"Suit yourself." She shrugged and disappeared in a flash of light.

"Show off," Val muttered. Although he could move much faster than a human, at nearly seven hundred years old Eone had perfected the ability to shift from one spot to another within seconds.

He realized Neil was frowning at him. "What?"

"You almost killed her."

He rolled his eyes. "Not even close, Neil. She

had plenty of blood left."

"Why did you take so much from her?"

"I was badly injured remember?"

"You didn't need to take that much." Neil gave him a look of disgust.

Val shrugged. "I'll apologize to her." He looked around. Most of the group was unloading the wagon but Abby was nowhere to be seen.

"She's in the house. Stay away from her, Val."

Val licked his lips. "She's not going to stay away from me, Neil. You know that."

"You don't have to make it any harder on her than it already will be. Avoid her as much as you can." He clapped Val on the shoulder and lifted a box of bedding from the back of the wagon.

Val grunted in reply and stared into the woods. He was hungry, despite the large amount of Abby's blood he had taken last night, but he didn't want deer. He wanted more of Abby. Her blood was deliciously sweet, and remembering the way she had moaned when he cupped her breast had his dick hardening in his pants.

He shook himself. He was being ridiculous. She was a chubby human who would most likely be dead within the month. The ones that came from her world never lasted long in his. Still, he couldn't help but remember the way her dark lashes had looked against the paleness of her skin. Her skin was so smooth and soft.

He swallowed thickly. She would not be able to resist him and when she came to him and begged him to touch and kiss her - to bite her - he would do it. He was doing the chubby human a favour really.

She would go mad if he didn't. He would drink her sweet blood each night and when they finally got back to civilization, they would dump her with the other humans and she would forget him.

❧ ❧

"Abby, do you want to share this room with me?" Maria examined the small bedroom. It had two twin beds in it and was obviously a bedroom for children.

Abby nodded as she peered into the room. "Why do you think this house was abandoned, Maria?"

Maria sighed. "Many of the houses in this area were abandoned when the leeches took over this part of the territory. It was quite a few years ago and their numbers have dwindled significantly since then, but most people never returned to their homes."

"Or they were killed by the vampires," David said.

"Aye, that's true," Maria agreed.

A shiver went through Abby. "Why are you travelling through here?"

David put down the bag he was carrying. "Our village was overtaken by the leeches. Those of us who escaped the carnage had no choice but to travel this way. We're going to Karna. It is a larger city and more secure."

Abigail frowned. There were only fifteen humans in the group and she had a sudden bad feeling. "How big was your village?"

David glanced at Maria. "There were over a

hundred of us."

"Oh my God," Abby whispered. "You're all that survived?"

Maria nodded and sat down on one of the beds. "It was a very large pod of leeches. If it hadn't been for Eone and Val, none of us would have lived."

"Is that why you're travelling with them?" Abigail asked. Her hand moved to her neck and she touched the two small holes on her throat.

Maria smiled at her. "Eone and Val have sworn allegiance to the humans. They have turned from their own kind and will never harm us."

"Why did they leave the other vampires?"

"Each of them has their own reason and it is not mine to share." Maria smiled at her before standing and clapping her hands briskly. "Enough talk for now. You need to have more to eat and drink. You're still much too pale."

She turned to David. "Will you keep an eye on her? Stay with her and help to distract her?"

"I don't need a babysitter." Abigail frowned.

"I know that," Maria replied. "But, Abby, please believe me when I tell you that you do not understand what will happen when you see Val. David is big and strong and will help you to stay away from Val, won't you, David?"

"Aye, I will," David replied solemnly.

"Why are you afraid of Val?" Maria asked suddenly. "Once a vampire has bitten a human, they're not usually afraid of them."

"I'm not afraid of him," Abigail lied. "He insulted me and nearly killed me by drinking too much. I don't want him near me again. And don't worry, I can control myself. Trust me."

"I know you believe that, Abby but…"

She trailed off and gave David a helpless look.

David took Abigail's hand in his. "Abigail, come to the kitchen with me and I'll make you some tea."

❧ ❧

He smelled her before he saw her. He inhaled deeply, a small smile playing on his lips, as the flow of her blood sang sweetly to him.

Patience, Val. She will come to you soon enough.

"Val?" Neil put his hand on his arm as he glanced past Val's shoulder. "Stay away from her. She's made it clear she doesn't want you to touch her again."

Val grinned at him, his fangs flashing in the dim light. "I will not have to go near her, Neil. She will come to me and I will not deny her what she wants."

"Why the sudden change? You were adamant yesterday that you wouldn't feed from her again."

Val shrugged. "Perhaps my time with the humans has returned a spark of my own humanity. I will feed from her like she will beg me to. I would think my decision would please you. Unless you want to watch the poor girl go mad?"

He could sense her in the room and he winked at Neil before turning around. He could feel his fangs lengthening in anticipation and he reminded himself to stay calm. Her blood was incredibly sweet, even frightened half to death. Tonight, he would seduce her and bring her pleasure and her blood would be unimaginably tastier. He could almost taste the thick, salty sweetness.

David was leading Abby into the room. He was gripping her hand y and nearly yanking her across the room toward the kitchen and Val grinned a little. He understood what the boy was trying to do but it was pointless. The moment Abigail saw him she would do whatever it took to get to him.

His smile widened when Abigail's head turned in his direction. She stared at him, her dark brown eyes sliding across his face before moving to Neil standing beside him. She smiled briefly at Neil and without hesitating followed David into the kitchen.

Val's mouth dropped open as Maria crossed the room and joined them. Her round face mirrored his own surprise and she stared at Neil.

"Did you see that?" She whispered.

Neil nodded as Val closed his mouth with a snap.

"Did she – did she just ignore me?" He could hardly spit the words out.

Neil burst into loud laughter and clapped Val so hard on the back the vampire staggered forward. "Welcome to my world, my blood-sucking friend."

"It is impossible. She should be - "

"Begging you to fuck her?" Neil asked crudely.

Maria slapped him lightly on the arm. "Don't be rude, Neil."

Val was staring at the kitchen doorway and spoke absentmindedly. "Perhaps it is because I did not seduce her first. Perhaps her fear from last night has somehow blocked her need for me."

Maria turned on him, her face red with fury. "You didn't calm her first? You bit her without using your powers to reassure and soothe her? You asshole!" She punched him hard on the chest. "Why would you do that to the poor girl? She offered to save your life and you repay her by biting into her while she was frightened and confused? Then you nearly killed her by drinking from her! You selfish fucking leech!"

"Maria, calm down." Neil pulled the small woman away from Val. She kicked him hard in the shin and he winced and let her go.

"She should have let you die, Val," she hissed at him before turning and stomping towards the kitchen.

Neil turned to him and Val actually felt a trickle of embarrassment at the look on the big man's face. "Why would you be so cruel to her, Val?"

"I don't know."

He was lying. He had done it because he was disgusted by the idea of a human pining after him despite her willingness to help him. Besides, he was so sure that her blood would taste horrible that he had just wanted to get it over with. Of course, that had changed the moment he had tasted her. Now he was craving her, and he never imagined that she would resist him.

"Do you really believe your cruelty is why she can resist you?" Neil asked curiously.

Val shook his head. "No. I have done this to other humans in the past and although it helped lessen their need a little, it did not diminish it completely."

He didn't know why Abigail could resist him but he was determined to find out.

∽ ∾

"Abigail? Are you okay?" Maria's warm hand touched her back hesitantly and Abby looked up from where she was staring at the kitchen table.

"Just fine."

Maria glanced at David. He was pouring water into a pot and he widened his eyes a little at her.

"I'm going to go put this over the fire in the fireplace," David said as he lifted the pot from the counter. "We'll have your tea ready in a bit, okay?"

"Okay," Abby said absently. She had returned to staring at the table.

"Abigail, you saw Val in the living room right?"

"Yes."

"And you felt nothing? No need for him?" Maria spoke hesitantly, as though even mentioning it would make it happen.

Abigail didn't reply and she reached out and tilted her face up. The girl's eyes were soft and unfocused and Maria frowned. "Abigail?"

Abby blinked rapidly. "I feel a bit of a draw to him," she admitted as she pressed her lips together. "But nothing I can't handle."

"Are you sure? Val has changed his mind about feeding from you again."

"Has he? How generous of him," Abigail said sarcastically.

"It will help. I know it was frightening for you last night but they do have the ability to make it -

well – less traumatizing. I'll get Neil to talk to Val about being gentler. And it will only be until we're in Karna. Once we're in the city it will be easier to avoid him, and the craving will wear off."

Abigail shook her head. "No. I don't need his pity feeding. I'm perfectly fine."

"Abby, what you're feeling right now will only get worse with time."

She frowned. "You said it would get better."

"Only if you're not around him," Maria replied patiently. "You will not be able to avoid him, and it will be at least another ten days before we get to Karna."

When Abigail didn't reply, Maria pressed her gently. "There is no shame in allowing him to feed from you, Abby. It is better than going mad with the need."

"I'm stronger than I look, Maria," Abigail said sharply. "Please will you go for a bit? I'd like to be alone."

Maria hesitated and then nodded. "All right."

As soon as she was gone, Abby grabbed the edge of the table until her knuckles turned white. She closed her eyes and breathed with deep flat inhales through her nose and soft, long exhales through her mouth.

Her entire body was throbbing and pulsing with the need to go to Val. She continued to hold the table, knowing it was the only thing that was stopping her from going to the arrogant vampire and asking him to fuck her. Asking him – hell, pleading with him - to bite her again.

Her pussy throbbed as she imagined lying on

her back and parting her thighs so Val could kneel between them. His cock would be big and thick and fill her completely. She knew that as well as she knew her own name. He would fuck her until she was begging to come and when he finally allowed her to, he would sink his fangs deep into her throat and the pleasure would intensify until she -

She was actually starting to stand when she got control of herself. She moaned low in her throat, resisting the urge to shove her hand down her pants and rub her clit. She bit the inside of her cheek until she could taste blood and forced herself to concentrate on her breathing.

She was looking for her place, the place that she had gone to most of her childhood and teenage years. It was safe and warm and after a few moments she slipped into it. The outside world faded away and she sat down in the warm grass and stared at the field of white daisies. The breeze blew and the petals rubbing together made a sound like soft whispering.

She had grown up in the foster system and spent most of her first few years being shuffled from home to home. When she was seven, she had been assigned to a foster home of an older couple. At first it had seemed wonderful but it had quickly turned into a horror show. The woman was a religious nut job and she had beaten and abused Abigail on a daily basis. She had threatened to kill Abby if she told her social worker and to avoid going insane, Abigail had created her safe place.

She supposed it was actually a sign of her own insanity that she could create a world so vivid and realistic but her safe place had saved her time and time again. The beatings, the hours of being forced on her knees in front of a large crucifix, all faded away when she was in her safe place. Even better, she would be calm and in control when she allowed herself to return to the real world.

There was no need to go to her internal world in years but now, as she sought it out with a desperation born of panic, she found it incredibly easy to return. Thoughts of Val faded away and her grip on the table loosened. She stared blankly across the room. A tiny part of her mind was aware of the soft murmuring of the others in the living room, of the fly that was buzzing at the window, but most of her consciousness was fully involved in her fantasy world.

When David returned, carrying a cup of steaming tea, she was sitting calm and relaxed in her chair. He crouched beside her and set the cup in front of her before touching her knee.

"Abby?"

She smiled down at him, her dark eyes hazy and far away. "Yes, David?"

"I brought you tea."

"Thank you."

"How are you feeling?"

"Fine, thank you."

He rubbed her large thigh, his hand tracing tiny circles on the top of it. She didn't seem to notice.

ॐ ॐ

Val stood in the doorway of the kitchen and frowned as David rubbed and circled Abigail's thigh. He had to control the urge to tear the man away from her and he scowled. What was happening to him?

"Abby, why don't you join us in the living room? We're going to be eating soon and - "

Abigail abruptly shuddered all over and in a low sing-song voice said, "He's here."

"Hello, Abigail." Val was suddenly standing next to them and David stood and moved protectively in front of Abby.

"Get out of here, Val."

"No."

David's hands clenched into fists and he glared at the larger man. "Get out now or I'll - "

"You'll what?" Val laughed, a deep rich sound, and held out his hands. "Do you really believe you have a chance against me?"

With terrifying quickness, he wrapped his hand around David's neck and lifted until the man was dangling in his grip. "You would be wise to not cross me, young David. I'm hungry and she has what I want."

David pulled futilely at Val's hand, his legs kicking as his face turned red.

"Let him go, Val." Her voice was soft but he dropped David immediately and turned to her, dismissing the boy completely.

"Of course, little dove."

He stood next to her and resisted the urge to stroke her long, dark hair. She had unbraided it and it fell halfway down her back in dark waves.

"Abby," David gasped out, his hand rubbing his throat, "come to the living room with me."

"Leave us, boy," Val said.

"Fuck you, leech," David spat.

"It's fine, David. You should go," Abby said in the same soft voice.

"Come with me," David pleaded.

She shook her head. "No, I'm fine."

Val's lips curved up in a smile of triumph as David flushed and strode jerkily from the room.

Abby was staring at the table in front of her and Val knelt at her feet. "Look at me, Abigail."

With a shuddering sigh she turned and stared at him. His blood pounded at the look of need in her eyes. She did want him after all, he could feel it radiating from her, and a trickle of relief went through him.

"Shall I feed from you now, sweet Abigail? Would you like that?" He murmured.

"So you can nearly kill me again?" The haze of desire lessened and he could see a small flicker of anger in her eyes.

He smiled at her. "I am sorry for that, my dove. I did not mean to take so much. I promise you it will not happen again."

She snorted. "And why should I trust you?"

He let his hand hover above her tightly-clasped hands. Christ, she was strong-willed. He had made a quick judgement of her in the forest and found her lacking. Now, watching as she fought her need for him, he could feel his admiration for her growing.

"I will never hurt you, Abigail. You're so beautiful."

"Liar," she whispered. "You think I'm fat and ugly. You said so last night, remember? You said you would not feed from me again because I was fat and tasted bad."

He winced. "I'm sorry, my dove. I was being an asshole. I should not have said that and I beg for your forgiveness. You're beautiful and taste delicious. I would very much like to taste you again."

"Tough titty said the kitty when the milk went dry," she said and he gave her an odd look.

"What does that mean?"

"It means get lost, scram, take a hike." She was breathing shallowly and her hands were squeezing the edge of the table compulsively.

His frustration grew and he reached out and cupped her face, knowing that his touch would be enough to convince her. She inhaled sharply and made a soft sound of need as her entire body shuddered.

"Look at me, Abigail," he commanded.

Her eyes lifted to his and he smiled. "That's right, my dove. See how much I want you, how much I need you."

His confident smile faded as the light disappeared from her eyes. She stared at him blankly and he frowned. "Abigail, can you hear me?"

She didn't reply and he stroked her face with his fingers. "Abigail? Say something."

She continued to ignore him. Her breathing was deep and even and she had gone limp in the chair. She was like a living, breathing doll and he frowned and snapped his fingers in front of her face.

"Abigail!" He said sharply and she jerked a

little.

"Go away, Val. I don't want you to feed from me," she sighed, her eyes still blank.

He gave a grunt of frustration and stalked from the room.

Chapter Four

"How is she doing it? Do you know?" Maria asked Neil.

It had been three days and they had spent the daylight hours traveling and their nights holed up in various houses. Tonight was the first night they had not found an abandoned house and they were forced to camp in the open. The entire group was tense and nervous and sticking close to the small, smokeless fire that Neil had built.

Neil shook his head. "I have no idea. I've never seen a human resist a vampire the way she does."

Maria hesitated. "It's like – I think – it's like she goes into herself. She's there but she's not there, you know? She disappears and shuts all of us out, but especially Val."

Neil nodded. "Yeah. It's driving Val crazy."

"It's driving her crazy too. She's slipping, Neil. She's built this iron-clad armor around herself but it's starting to break apart. She's hardly sleeping and she doesn't have much of an appetite. If David and I didn't watch her and remind her to eat, I don't think she would eat at all."

"Why won't she let him feed from her?" Neil asked.

"Probably because he was an asshole and frightened her the first time he fed."

Neil shook his head. "He's been actively trying to seduce her for the last three days. That should have overridden her fear."

"We have to do something," Maria said desperately. "I'll speak to her again, try and convince her to - "

"No, don't." David sat down beside them. "It's admirable what she's doing. Those damn leeches think they can do whatever they want with us, and she's showing them we can't be controlled."

Maria frowned at him. "At what cost? Her sanity? She's cracking under the pressure, David."

"She's fine," David said dismissively.

"No, she isn't!" Maria snapped.

"Whatever, Maria. You don't even know her."

"And you think you do?"

"I've been spending lots of time with her the last three days. We talk and I help her to ignore that asshole leech in the evenings. She's a good, sweet girl and she doesn't need to be corrupted any further by him."

He stood and walked around the fire to Abby. He sat down on the log beside her and dropped his arm across her shoulders. She gave him a tired, distracted smile before staring back at the flames.

"Someone has a crush," Neil said dryly.

Maria sighed. "David hates the vampires, Neil.

He always has and he always will. Does he have a crush on her or is he using her to drive Val mad?"

"I don't know, but he's the least of our concerns. We need to try and convince Abby to allow Val to feed from her."

"Yeah." Maria looked around. "Where is Val anyway?"

"He went hunting tonight with Eone. He's been holding off, convinced that he would feed from Abigail, but he couldn't hold out any longer."

☙ ❧

Abigail stood, rubbing at her forehead, and David immediately stood with her.

"Where are you going?"

She tamped down the twinge of irritation she felt at his nosiness and forced herself to smile at him. "I need to use the bathroom."

"I'll come with you."

"No, you will not." She scowled at him. "I'm quite capable of peeing by myself, thanks."

She walked away before he could protest and disappeared into the trees. She walked a few feet until she was hidden from the campsite and pulled her pants down. She reached into her pocket and pulled out the small amount of soft paper that Maria had given her for this very purpose before squatting and peeing. She couldn't believe how quickly she had adjusted to peeing on the ground.

She stood and pulled up her pants. She hesitated – she didn't want to go back to the camp, not yet. The voices of the others, their very presence, was annoying her more and more. What did she care about their idle chatter or their attempts at friendship when thoughts of Val drummed steadily in her head?

She rubbed at her forehead again. Maria was right – it was getting worse. Hardly a moment went by where she wasn't thinking about Val. When she wasn't wondering what it would be like to kiss him, to have his strong hands on her naked breasts, and to feel his fangs in her flesh once more. To make matters worse, every time she turned around he was there, staring at her with those silvery grey eyes that practically dripped sex. She knew without a doubt that he was trying to seduce her, and he was doing a remarkable job.

She could hardly remember the pain of his first feeding. All she could picture now was his hard hand squeezing her breast and his thigh pushing against her core. When he looked at her, his eyes promised long nights of unimaginable pleasure and she desperately wanted to give in to him.

She released a long, shuddering breath. It was getting more and more difficult to slip into her safe place. The sound of Val's deep voice or an image of the dark shadow on his jaw would cut into her thoughts just as she was sitting down in the field of flowers, and she would be ripped out of her dream world just like that.

She should have been freaking out about being whisked to some other version of earth by a giant glowing orb. She should have been giving some thought to how she might return to her own world, but none of that seemed to matter. The only thing that mattered was Val.

Why are you torturing yourself like this, Abby? He wants you and you want him. Let him take what he wants. He promised he wouldn't hurt you and maybe then you could get some sleep. Let him feed from you just once. There's no harm in allowing him to take a small amount. And I bet if you begged sweetly enough, he'd fuck you with that big, hard cock. He could –

She shook her head. Val had insulted her in front of a room full of people she had just met and told Neil and Eone to leave her in the forest to die. She hated him.

She let him feed from her once because she owed him a debt. She had paid it in full and she owed him nothing now. If she could get through nearly twelve years of abuse and psychotic raving from her foster mother, she could get through this. Only another week or so and they would be in Karna, and she would never have to see him again. She would concentrate on finding a way home.

A small flickering light caught her eye and she frowned and moved further into the woods. Her breath caught in her throat when she saw the tiny creature struggling silently in a large web strung across the low branches of a tree.

She moved closer and inspected the struggling creature. It was female with long violet-coloured hair and a slim body covered in a wisp of green fabric. Her skin was a rich, dark purple and she was glowing brightly. She was about the length of a butter knife and the tiny creature grimaced at her as she twisted and turned in the sticky web. Abby realized with a numb type of surprise that large, nearly invisible wings sprouted from its back. The wings were currently tucked against her tiny body. Strands of the web crisscrossed her body firmly and the more she struggled, the tighter they tangled about her.

"You poor thing," Abigail murmured. She was reaching to help the tiny creature when Eone spoke from her left.

"Leave it, Abby."

She gasped and whirled around, dropping her eyes immediately to the ground when she realized Val was standing next to Eone. It was better, easier, to resist him if she didn't look at him.

"What is it?" She whispered, turning to stare at the creature still struggling in the web.

"She's a pixie," Eone said carelessly. She moved forward and glanced at it. "She flew too close to the web and will soon be the spider's next meal."

Abigail frowned. "We have to help her."

Eone laughed. "Pixie's are rotten little creatures, Abby. Trust me, there is no shortage of them and one less in the world will be a blessing. She'll probably bite you the minute you free her anyway. They hate humans."

"So that means I should leave her to die?" Abby glared at her.

"Eone's right," Val spoke quietly from behind her. "Pixies are never alone. The fact that none of her own kind have come forward to help her, means there is something wrong with her. Leave her to her fate."

Eone took her arm and began to lead her away

from the pixie. "Come, Abby. It is not safe for you to be here in the woods alone."

With a surprising show of strength, Abigail pulled her arm free and darted back to the spider's web. Before Eone or Val could stop her, she had ripped the pixie free of the web. Carrying her loosely in one hand, she marched back to the campsite.

She sat down on the log beside the fire and began to carefully untangle the long strands of web from the pixie's small body. The pixie lay silently in her hand, staring distrustfully at her as the others gathered around.

"Ugh. A pixie." Erin's nose wrinkled with disgust. "They're such vile little things."

Maria sat down beside her. "Where did you find it?"

"It was trapped in a spider's web," Abby said distractedly. She was trying to remove the sticky web from the delicate wings and she was worried that she would tear the wing right from her back.

The pixie winced and her mouth opened in pain but no sound came out.

"I'm sorry, little one," Abigail whispered.

"Here." Maria had left and returned with a damp cloth. Abigail swiped it gently across the pixie's wings. It helped to loosen the web, and she carefully peeled the strands away from her wings before starting to work on the sticky strands that bound her arms and legs.

"You should have left it in the web to die." Bert peered at the pixie disinterestedly. "They're nothing but pests."

"Be quiet, Bert!" Menora, a soft and quiet woman who hadn't said more than five words to Abby, said sharply. "You're such a dick sometimes."

Landon spoke from his spot by the fire. "I've heard that pixies are good luck."

"They're not," David said flatly. "Bert's right – they're annoying pests."

Abigail ignored them all and continued to unwind the strands from the pixie. After about fifteen minutes, the small creature was completely free of the strands. She laid quietly in the palm of Abby's hand and Abby frowned.

"Maybe she needs some water. She was struggling so much. She must be thirsty."

Without speaking Neil brought her a cup of water and Abby dipped her finger into it. She held it over the pixie and let a small drop splash onto her face. The pixie flinched and glared at her.

"I'm sorry." Abby smiled at her. "I thought you might be thirsty."

The pixie stood up, her bare feet resting steadily against Abby's palm, and cupped her hands. Abigail dipped her finger into the cup of water again and shook another drop of water from her finger into the pixie's hands. The pixie drank from her cupped hands, and Abigail gasped with delight when she shook herself and her wings unfurled from her body.

She fluttered them rapidly back and forth and her body rose a few inches from Abby's palm. She hovered like a humming bird for a second or two as her tiny body began to glow, and then suddenly darted into the night sky. She rose higher and Abby followed the tiny glowing light until it disappeared into the trees.

"Ungrateful little slug," Bert said but Abigail just shrugged and turned back to staring into the fire. The pixie had driven thoughts of Val from her mind for the first time in days, but already she could feel him squirming back into her brain like an itch she couldn't scratch.

Oh he could scratch that itch for you, make no mistake about that.

She shuddered and stared moodily at the small golden flames. Only another week – she could do this.

Chapter Five

"You have a secret admirer." Neil nudged her as she walked steadily behind the wagon. Her thighs hurt and her back hurt from the four straight days of walking but she ignored it grimly. It would have been a lot worse if she hadn't been exercising for a few months before she was sucked from her world into this one.

"What are you talking about?" She lifted her face to the late afternoon sunshine and ignored the small voice that urged her to climb into the compartment below the wagon and join Val in his slumber.

"Look to your left, quickly."

She looked and blinked in surprise when she saw the tiny pixie dart out of sight behind a large bush dotted with orange berries.

"How long has she been there?" She wondered aloud.

Neil shrugged. "I noticed her about an hour ago."

"Why won't she come over to me?" Abby

asked.

"Frankly, I'm surprised she's even following you. Pixies really dislike humans."

"Why?"

"I don't know. Maybe because we treat them like pests."

"Val said they travel in packs."

"Aye, normally. If you find one alone it's usually because something's wrong with it and the others have driven it from the pack. To be honest, she won't survive long on her own."

Abigail frowned. "Poor little thing."

Neil patted her on the shoulder. "You gave her a chance at least."

"I guess."

"May I speak with you about something, Abby?" Neil asked.

She looked at him curiously. For the first time all day, David had left her side, joining Landon and Bert in a lively discussion about something called barnen. From what she could tell, it was some sort of card game and they seemed to take it very seriously.

"What is it?"

Neil stared at her gravely. "You should let Val feed from you."

She stiffened and turned away. "No. He insulted me and told you to leave me in the forest to die."

"He also saved your life in that forest," Neil reminded her gently.

"And I paid him back for that by saving his life," she spat. "I owe him nothing."

"I know." Neil patted her shoulder soothingly. "You should let him feed from you not because you owe him something but because frankly, you're going mad."

"I am not. I'm just tired," she denied.

"Abby, it's amazing that you've lasted this long but you can't keep this up. You'll go insane before we reach Karna."

"I appreciate your concern but you don't know me, Neil. You have no idea how strong I actually am. I'll make it to Karna just fine."

"I've spoken with Val. I know he was – was cruel earlier but he feels bad about that and wants the chance to make it up to you. He will be gentle and only take enough of your blood to soothe your need."

She laughed. "He feels bad? Tell me, Neil, how exactly does a bloodsucking soulless leech *feel bad*?"

"Vampires have souls, Abby."

Abby frowned at him. "No, they don't. All the books and TV shows say they don't."

"TV?" Neil looked at her doubtfully.

"Never mind." She shook her head impatiently. "They don't have souls, and they don't feel remorse or love or gratitude. They're dead. They have no heartbeat and no ability to feel the way we do. Everyone knows that."

"You're wrong, Abby. Vampires have hearts that beat just like humans and they are capable of feeling every emotion that humans do. I have seen it for myself."

Abigail blinked in tired surprise. "In my world,

they're the undead. Their hearts no longer beat and they have no souls."

Neil smiled a little. "Your world sounds like an awful place to live."

She shook her head. "It isn't. It's perfectly wonderful and besides, vampires don't actually exist in my world. They're a – a fairy tale."

"How strange. Believe me, Abby, the reason that humans hate the vampires is because they feed from us like cattle and look at us as nothing more than toys for their amusement. Humans don't fear them because they're the undead. Although I will admit that Eone and Val are kinder to humans than most vampires are," Neil murmured.

He hesitated and then tried again. "Val is not the monster you think, Abigail. Let him feed - "

"Fine, they have souls and feelings and blah, blah, blah. I don't care. Val is an asshole. If he feels so bad and wants to help, tell him to stay away from me then. I don't need him staring at me every time I turn around," she said grumpily.

"He already is," Neil pointed out. "Did you not notice the way he avoided you last night?"

She shook her head. She had spent most of the evening after the pixie had flown away, hovering in her dream world. Her need for Val was almost undeniable last night.

"He did." Neil stared at the tracks the wagon wheels were leaving in the soft dirt. He'd been shocked when Val hadn't tried to seduce Abby last night. He had known the vampire for many years and not once had Val ever put the needs of a human over his own needs. He took what he wanted regardless of the consequences. The fact that he had gone hunting and drank deer blood instead of just taking what he wanted from Abby was astonishing.

Remembering how she had saved the pixie last night, he tried a different route, hoping to appeal to her obvious desire to help others. "You are not the only one who suffers, Abby. Val suffers too. I have never seen him yearn for a human the way he does you."

She hesitated and he felt a brief glimmer of hope before her face set back into a stubborn scowl.

"Let him suffer."

&ro &6

Val's eyes opened the moment the wagon stopped. He could sense the light and waited impatiently for it to fade from the sky. His thoughts turned to Abigail like they always did, and a combination of need and worry flowed through him. What had started off as an obsession for her blood had evolved over the last few days into an obsession with her.

Although he desperately wanted to taste her blood again, he also wanted to be with her. He was shocked to realize he thought her to be one of the most beautiful humans he had ever seen. Her dark eyes and hair, her pale skin, had him half-hard every time he was around her. David was already half in love with her. He could understand why. She was sweet and kind-hearted and, despite her obvious confusion about what was happening, she was gamely trying to make the best of her new life.

She hadn't eaten at all last night. Normally David or Maria made sure she ate but they were distracted by the pixie. If he wasn't making a conscious effort to try and help her sanity by staying away from her, he would have brought her food and made her eat it. He had finally gone to Maria and told her, but it was late by then and Abigail had refused to eat.

He sighed. Even after only a few days she had lost weight. Too big to begin with, her borrowed pants were noticeably larger and her t-shirt didn't hug her curves nearly as much. He took a deep breath as he pictured her large breasts. He wanted to strip her naked, kiss every part of her body and make her come repeatedly. He wanted to shove his cock deep inside of her and feel her warmth gripping him as he plunged in and out of her tight pussy.

His cock hardened and throbbed in his pants and he released his breath in a long, drawn-out hiss. Eone turned to face him, her eyes drifting down his body, and a small sound of excitement escaped her throat.

She curled up to him and put her hand on his dick, rubbing and squeezing it through his pants. "Do you want to, Val? It's been years since we've mated but I'm not entirely opposed to the idea of fucking you again."

He knocked her hand away with a low snarl. "Get away from me, Eone."

"Fine," she said huffily. "You don't have to be such a dick about it."

He didn't reply as he listened to Neil

approaching the compartment. The door swung open and he slid out, his eyes searching the dim light for Abigail. She was standing a few feet from the others, staring hypnotized at the large pink flower that was opening in front of her.

Horror rushed through him and he shouted her name as he flew lightning-quick across the clearing.

❧ ❦

Abby sighed and bent over, stretching her aching back. They had stopped for the night and she was glad that she would soon be off her sore feet, but the setting sun meant that Val would be waking from his daysleep. She shivered and closed her eyes.

Please let him stay away from me tonight. I don't have the strength to resist him anymore.

She straightened and glanced around. They had found a small house with an even smaller barn nestled behind it. The others were carrying the supplies into the house, and she was reaching for a bag from the wagon when the flower caught her eye.

She turned and stared at it. It was a large, pink flower on a thick green stalk. It waved in the slight breeze as if beckoning to her, and she realized with sweet wonderment that its petals were opening up. What kind of flower opened at night, she wondered briefly. She walked toward it and leaned over, staring intently into the center of the flower. A strange, not unpleasant smell, was drifting from it and she could see small red stalks unfolding from the middle of its soft petals.

"So beautiful," she murmured and leaned closer.

She heard Val shout her name as the red stalks shot their tiny spears directly into her throat. There were tiny pinpricks of pain and then Val was standing beside her, his strong arm around her shoulders, and he was pulling her away from the flower and yanking the spears from her throat.

"Abigail! Abigail! Stay awake!" He shouted at her.

The light was dimming and her eyelids were growing incredibly heavy. A strange paralysis crept over her body and with the last of her strength she clawed at Val's face. She tried to say his name but nothing passed her lips but a soft whispering moan. The last thing she saw before the darkness claimed her was Val's pale and worried face.

৵ ৶

"What do we do?" Val shouted at Neil. He was sitting on the ground cradling Abigail and he gave Neil a look of pure panic.

His face pale, Neil shook his head. "There's nothing we can do, Val. The flower's poison has already entered her blood stream. She'll be dead within the hour."

Val growled at him and pulled Abigail closer before staring at the others. "One of you useless humans must know an antidote, a way to save her."

When they didn't reply he gave a scream of rage and anger that made them all wince. David approached and Val snarled, "Do not touch her!"

David backed away as Val stared down at Abby's face. He brushed her hair back from her smooth skin and rocked her back and forth. "Wake up, little dove," he whispered pleadingly.

Maria knelt beside him and took Abigail's hand. Already it was growing cold as the poison worked its way through her body.

"Val," she spoke hesitantly. "You could turn her."

"No! I will not do that to her."

"She's dying, Val," Maria said.

"Maria's right." Eone crouched beside them. "If you want her to live, then turn her."

"That's not living!" Val hissed at her. "Besides, I cannot turn her from my bite alone. She must drink my blood. How are we supposed to make her drink?"

"Pour it down her throat. It will work well enough." Eone shrugged carelessly. "Or don't. It matters not to me if the human lives or dies."

"There must be another way." Val gave Neil and Maria a stricken look.

"There isn't," Maria said. "There is no antidote for the flower's poison. You know that, Val."

He stared down at her and placed his hand on her chest. Already he could feel her heartbeat slowing and her breathing was shallow and too slow. He gave a low cry of distress and opened his mouth, letting his fangs extend as he tilted her head back.

Before he could plunge his fangs into her throat, there was a sharp stinging pain as something bit his earlobe. He jerked as the pixie flew past his face. She was giving him a furious look and she bit him on the nose before dropping down and landing on

Abigail's shoulder.

"Get away from her, bug!" He reached to flick her away and she immediately tangled herself in Abigail's long dark hair.

"Stop it!" He poked at her and gave a low mutter of pain when she bit him on the tip of his finger. Her teeth were small but needle sharp, and a drop of blood fell before his body quickly healed itself.

She bared her teeth at him in a silent snarl before cautiously untangling herself from Abigail's hair.

"Leave her," Maria said.

"She's dying," Val gritted out. "I need to turn her before it's too late."

"Give her a minute," Maria insisted.

The others crowded around, watching curiously as the little pixie hovered above Abigail's face. She patted Abigail's cheek with her hands, and then pressed her mouth against Abby's lower lip before flying down and landing on her collarbone.

She leaned forward, her hands on her hips and her wings vibrating, and studied the marks from the spears on Abby's neck. She straightened and rose a few inches in the air until she was hovering over Abigail's neck, directly above the marks. They were bright red and Val could see the red lines of infection already spreading across her pale throat.

"What's she doing?" Neil whispered.

"I don't know," Maria said.

The pixie stared briefly at Val before spinning around to face Abigail. She clapped her hands together in a quick, steady rhythm.

Val frowned. "What - "

Maria gasped when the glitter-like substance fell from the pixie's rhythmically-clapping hands. It settled like dust onto Abby's throat and the marks were quickly buried beneath the lightly-glowing dust. The pixie clapped harder. Her wings fluttered until they were nothing but a blur, and her tiny body was glowing so brightly that it cast a dim light over the entire group.

Val jerked in surprise when Abigail twitched in his arms and gave a sharp, shuddering gasp. The pixie smiled and stopped clapping her hands. She flew a few feet away and hovered, watching as Val brushed the pixie dust from Abby's throat.

Maria sucked in her breath. "Oh my God."

The marks from the spears were gone as were the red lines of infection. Val glanced at the pixie. She was giving him a smug look of satisfaction and stuck her tongue out at him.

He ignored her and cupped Abby's face. "Abigail, can you hear me?"

Her eyelids fluttered and she opened her eyes and stared at him.

"How do you feel, little dove?"

For the first time in days, she was staring directly at him and not fading into herself. He smiled at her and she gave him a sweet smile in return.

"Val," she sighed his name and her hand came up to grip the back of his neck. "Kiss me, please."

She tugged on his neck and he bent his head and pressed his mouth against hers. She moaned into his mouth and when he ran his tongue across her lips, she parted them eagerly. He was just sliding his tongue into her mouth when she was hauled from his arms. His fangs tore at her mouth, and she gave a sharp cry of pain mixed with frustration as David dragged her away from him. Val leaped to his feet. There was a single drop of her blood on his lip and he licked it away, his body shuddering at the sweet taste, before he snarled and bared his fangs at the man.

"Give her back to me now or I'll kill you where you stand, human."

"No." David was afraid, Val could smell it coming off of him in slow waves, but he tightened his arm around Abby's shoulders as she leaned against him and touched her bleeding mouth.

"Little dove, I'm sorry." He didn't take his eyes from David's. "I did not mean to hurt you."

"It's fine. I – I'm fine," she stuttered.

"Good." He turned his gaze to her and held his hand out. "Come to me, Abigail."

She took a step forward, her gaze burning into his, and then David was pulling her back. "No, Abby. Stay strong."

She shook her head at the sound of David's voice and the spell between them was broken. "Please, can I lie down? I'm very tired."

"Of course." David began to help her walk to the house and Val hissed with fury. He'd had enough of David's interference. He would kill the human and be done with it. Neil's hard hand fell on his arm.

"Don't, Val."

Val glanced down at Neil's hand and although

he could have ripped off the man's arm with little effort, he allowed him to pull him to a stop.

"If you kill him, she'll never let you touch her again. You know that. Use your head."

Chapter Six

Abigail sat cross-legged on the bed and touched the cut on her lip. She had nearly died, been healed by a pixie and kissed Val. Kissing Val was the only thing that she cared about. She sighed and stared out the window into the darkness. David had wanted to stay with her but after half an hour she had asked him to leave.

She hadn't wanted to hurt his feelings but she could feel her anger throbbing and burning inside of her. If it hadn't been for him, she would be with Val right now. He would be between her legs, his cock easing the ache between her thighs, and his fangs easing the ache in her brain.

Later, when she had gotten control of herself, she would be grateful to David but right now she wanted to scream with frustration and rage. She touched her mouth again, remembering how it felt to have Val's firm lips on hers. She had expected them to be cold but they weren't. They were warm and had started a thirst in her veins that only he could quench.

She breathed in and out for a few moments before a light outside of the window caught her attention. The pixie hovered outside and Abby didn't hesitate. She ran across the room and opened the window. The pixie flew in and stared nervously at her.

"Hello, little one. Thank you for saving my life," Abby said. Moving slowly, she sat down cross-legged on the bed, secretly delighted when the pixie followed her and landed on her knee. She mimicked Abby's posture, planting her small butt on Abby's leg and crossing her long purple limbs.

"What's your name, little one?" Abby asked.

The pixie cocked her head at her but didn't reply.

"Can you speak?"

The pixie shook her head before opening her mouth and making a fluttering gesture along her throat and in front of her open mouth with her hands. She made desperate grabbing motions before heaving a sigh and hanging her head.

"Was your voice stolen from you?" Abby frowned.

The pixie nodded gravely.

"Is that why your own kind rejected you?"

The pixie made a delicate shrugging motion and stared bored at the ceiling.

"I wonder what your name is," Abby said. "Maybe I could guess it."

The pixie jumped to her feet, her wings fluttering, and gestured excitedly at Abigail.

"Okay, okay. Let me try. Hmm... is it Gertrude?"

Abigail laughed when the pixie gave her a look of horror and crossed her arms in a huff.

"Not Gertrude. How about Mabel?"

This time the pixie stomped her feet and turned away. Abby touched her back delicately with her finger and the tiny creature faced her once more.

"I'm sorry for teasing you, little one. Let me try again. Is it Sara? Melody? Madison? Vanessa?"

The pixie shook her head at each name and Abigail blurted, "Tinkerbell?"

The pixie rolled her eyes and made a gagging motion. Abigail laughed again. "It's hopeless, little one. I'll never figure it out."

The pixie stared thoughtfully at her for a moment and then held up her hand in a "watch me" gesture. Abigail watched as the pixie mimed something out on her leg. Her tired mind, still clanging dully with thoughts of Val, had to watch it several times. The pixie repeated the motions patiently until the light bulb went on in Abby's brain.

"Flowers! You're picking flowers!"

The pixie nodded and clapped her hands excitedly, bouncing up and down on Abby's leg.

"Is your name Flower?" Abigail asked.

The pixie shook her head and made a try again motion.

You're named after a flower?" Abby said slowly after a few minutes.

The pixie nodded again and then stroked her long purple hair before pointing at the skin on her bare thigh.

Abby frowned as she did it again and again.

Her eyes widened. "Your name is Violet!"

This time the pixie shot into the air and twirled with glee in front of Abigail. Her tiny body glowed brightly and a small smatter of glowing pixie dust sprinkled down from her and landed on Abby's bare arm. The arm tingled pleasantly for a few seconds.

Abby held out her finger. "I'm Abigail. It's nice to meet you, Violet."

The pixie flew forward, grasped Abby's finger in her small hand and shook it.

✎ ✎

Abby sighed and sank into the soft grass. The white daisies nodded back and forth and she lifted her face to the warm sunshine. She looked dreamily at the clouds that dotted the sky like small puffs of smoke. She could feel her body relaxing and she closed her eyes. She was so tired.

A shadow fell across her face. Val stood before her. He was naked and her eyes dropped to his erect cock. Warmth flooded through her pelvis and belly and she moaned when he knelt in front of her and pushed her gently onto her back.

"Open your legs, little dove," he murmured. She stared into his eyes and let her legs part. He nestled his body into the cradle of her hips and at the first feel of his cock against her pussy, she arched upward. She was as naked as he and she tried to remember when she had taken off her clothes. Had it been before or after she went to her safe place?

She put her thighs around his waist and he smiled at her, his fangs flashing in the sunlight. As he sunk his cock deep inside of her, he lowered his mouth to her throat. She lifted her chin, gasping at the feel of his hardness throbbing inside of her. His mouth nuzzled her neck and her nipples turned to hard pebbles when his teeth touched against her skin. He opened his mouth and –

Abigail gasped and tore herself out of her dream world. She sat up from her blankets on the floor, shuddering and shaking and moaning quietly. Val had found her safe place. He had found her safe place and she was going to go mad and –

She was hyperventilating. Her head was buzzing and she felt faint. Quickly, she bent over and stuck her head between her legs, forcing herself to breathe deeply.

Breathe. Breathe. Just breathe, Abigail. Just breathe.

After about five minutes, she was calmer and she raised her head cautiously and looked around the small bedroom. The house was small and all of the women had crammed into the one room to sleep. She turned her head to the left. She had made Violet a bed out of small scraps of fabric, and the pixie had burrowed herself so far under them that only the top of her head was showing.

The buzzing in her brain had stopped but her pussy was throbbing and pulsing to the point of pain. Her fantasy about fucking Val had left her wet and dripping. She eased her hand under the blankets and stopped when Erin made a soft, snorting noise in her sleep.

She couldn't masturbate in this room full of women. She was so turned on that when she came there would be no way to hold in her moans of pleasure. Hell, moans? The way she felt right now, she would be screaming. She pushed back the covers and stood, creeping past the sleeping women and slipping silently out of the bedroom.

There was no place in the house she could go. Her fists curled in frustration as she tried to think past the need that was making her entire body vibrate. The barn. She would go to the barn and alleviate some of this pulsing need. If she didn't, she really would go crazy.

It took her less than five minutes to slip out of the house and enter the barn. The horses were in two of the stalls and they snorted sleepily at her as she moved past them to the third and empty stall. There was a blanket folded over the side of the stall and she shook it out quickly and laid it across the ground. She was wearing panties and a long shirt and she stared down at the blanket before suddenly shoving her hand inside her panties. She leaned against the stall, her breath coming in soft gasps and moans, as she rubbed and stroked her clit rapidly. She slid two fingers into her tight pussy, gasping Val's name as she used her thumb to rub her throbbing clit.

&ref; &ref;

Val walked slowly through the barn, his eyes glued to Abigail's trembling back. The horses neighed nervously and shied away from him but he paid them no attention and neither did Abby. Although her lower half was hidden by the walls of the stall he knew she was touching herself. His cock was hard and throbbing and he adjusted himself through his pants, trying to relieve some of the pressure.

When he had seen her sneaking into the barn, her white shirt glowing in the darkness, he had automatically assumed she was meeting someone. David, no doubt. He had seen it before in humans who lusted after a vampire. If they could not have the vampire, they would fuck as many humans as they could in a vain attempt to quell the urges inside of them.

His blood had boiled at the thought of David touching her and he had entered the barn quickly, ready to tear the man off of her. Relief had coursed through him when he realized she was alone. The relief was buried beneath a hard throb of lust when she uttered his name in a soft little moan.

He entered the stall behind her and although he was completely silent, her back stiffened. She knew he was there, every nerve in her body was highly attuned to him, and she gave a soft moan of dismay but kept her hand between her legs.

"Go away," she gasped, her hand rubbing furiously.

He pressed against her, his cock pushing against her ass as he reached around her and cupped her heavy breasts through her shirt. She cried out and tore her hand free of her panties. She clutched the side of the stall with both hands, he could see her juices glistening on her fingers, and he pinched her hard nipples between his thumbs and forefingers.

"Val!" She cried and pushed back against him, rubbing her ass against his cock and arching her back.

"Let me help you, little dove," he whispered into her ear. "Let me take away some of your need."

"I don't need your help," she moaned as he reached down and stroked one pale thigh before slipping his hand under her shirt. His fingers traced the waistband of her panties before he moved them under the elastic. He let his hand rest against her round stomach as he sucked on her earlobe.

"You do, little dove. You're wet and aching, and you need my cock. I can feel how much you need it."

He moved his hand down further until his fingers touched the soft curls at the apex of her thighs. She clamped her legs together and he once again admired her willpower. He used his other hand to turn her face toward his and he smiled at her before kissing her. His tongue swept through her mouth, searching and tasting and she returned his kiss eagerly.

He sucked on her lower lip, his tongue running over the small cut on it before he released it with a soft pop. She was panting and staring at him. Her cheeks were flushed with colour and she was rubbing her ass repeatedly against him without realizing it.

"I don't want the others to know that I let you," she panted.

"I won't feed from you, Abigail," he said suddenly.

She swallowed. "Do you promise?"

"Yes, I promise. I will not bite until you ask me

to bite you." He smiled reassuringly at her.

"I won't ask you," she whispered.

He said nothing. She would ask him to bite her, she would beg for it in fact, and he would not be able to resist her pleas. But he could help her by biting her in places easily concealed.

"Open your legs, little dove," he encouraged and she gave him a startled look before relaxing her legs just a fraction. He pushed them apart. She was so wound up she would come, and come loudly, the moment he touched her. He slammed his mouth down on hers as his fingers touched her clit. She screamed into his mouth as she came violently against his hand. He wrapped one arm tight around her waist, holding her up when her knees gave out and she collapsed against him.

He turned her to face him and pulled her shirt over her head. He lowered her onto her back on the blanket and pulled off her panties. Already her hand was moving back between her thighs, her fingers pushing past her wet lips to rub at her clit once more. She had waited too long and he would have to make her come multiple times before the fire in her belly for him was extinguished. He smiled. He was more than up to the task at hand.

&» «&

Abby knew she should be embarrassed. She had come explosively with only a single touch from Val, and he had stripped her naked and lowered her to the ground without a word of protest from her. She had thought that coming would bring some relief but it had only seemed to make it worse. She couldn't stop herself from reaching between her legs as the blanket scratched roughly at her back and ass. He pulled her hand away and she slapped at him, mewling with need and frustration. He grinned and pulled off his shirt before lying down between her thighs.

"Cover your mouth, little dove," he whispered before his tongue slicked across her clit. She bucked her hips and threw her arm over her mouth, screaming once more as she came hard again.

Even before she had finished he was parting her lips with his long fingers and licking her cream away. His tongue probed her tight opening and she moaned his name. He pushed her thighs wide and began his sweet, sensual assault once more.

She lost track of how many times he brought her to orgasm. By the time he pushed off his pants and propped himself above her, his face was soaked with her juices and the need that was driving her nearly mad had lost its edge.

She still wanted him, needed to feel his cock inside of her, but she no longer thought she might go crazy. He smiled at her and her gaze dropped to his fangs. They were long and glistening and her pelvis arched as she thought about them sinking into her soft flesh. There would be pain, but it would be a sweet pain, she thought dimly.

"Are you ready, my sweet dove?" He whispered.

"Yes," she murmured. "Please fuck me, Val. Please."

He pushed his cock into her, both moaning as he slid into her tight, wet pussy. She wrapped her legs around his waist, hooking her feet into the small of his back as he thrust slowly in and out of her.

"You feel so good, Abigail," he groaned. "So warm, so wet."

He leaned down and, for the first time, took her nipple into his mouth. He teased it with his tongue, feeling it harden in his mouth. He kept his fangs away from her nipple and sucked hard. Her hands gripped his head as her hips twitched and jerked against him and she came helplessly around his hard cock. He smiled down at her and continued to plunge in and out of her as she gasped and moaned beneath him. The warmth was growing within her again and she urged him to move faster.

He shook his head. "No, Abigail. You don't get to come again until I let you."

"Please, Val," she panted. "Please..."

"You don't like this?" He whispered. "Should I stop?" He pulled out of her, resting the head of his cock against her opening, and she cried out with frustration.

"No!" She clutched at his rock-hard biceps. "Please don't stop! I need your cock. I need it so much."

"I know, little dove," he said soothingly as he slid his cock back into her.

Abigail moaned. His cock was as hard and thick as she had imagined it to be. Each time he pushed into her, it filled her wet pussy completely and she quivered helplessly under him.

As he slowly pushed in and out of her, the fire grew in her until she was devoured by it. She couldn't stop staring at his mouth and when he dipped his head and took her nipple into his mouth, she twisted against him, trying to scrape his teeth against her.

He lifted his head, his eyes dark with lust. "Naughty girl. I almost bit you when you did that."

She took a deep shuddering breath and the plea was coming out of her mouth before she could stop it. "Please bite me, Val. Please."

He didn't make her beg. He couldn't have even if he wanted to. His need for her blood consumed him and he thrust rapidly in and out of her as he plunged his fangs deep into her shoulder. She cried out and her pussy clamped down around him as her orgasm burst through her and her blood filled his mouth in a sweet hot rush. He drank deeply as his entire body shuddered and he climaxed hard within her.

Abigail cried out again as her orgasm radiated through her. The pain from Val's bite had faded quickly and she was having her strongest climax yet. It radiated from her pelvis through her entire body, and with one final shouting gasp she arched her hips against his and passed out.

Chapter Seven

"Wake up, little dove. Please."

His voice whispered in her ear and she blinked and stared blankly at the ceiling of the barn. Val's face, lined with worry, appeared over her.

"I fed too much."

She shook her head. "No, you didn't. I didn't, uh, pass out from lack of blood."

He stared puzzled at her for a moment and she blushed when he suddenly grinned widely.

"Stop looking so smug," she muttered.

He laughed and kissed the tip of her nose. His hard chest was rubbing against her breasts and she was dismayed to feel a familiar tingle starting in her pelvis again. She should have been sated. She had come multiple times, the last one so intense she had passed out, but already she could feel the need for him starting up again.

She squirmed a little, trying to put some space between them, and he frowned and pressed his upper body against hers. "Where are you going?"

"I should go back to the house," she said. "It's

late."

"Not that late. There is still plenty of time left."

"Plenty of time left for what?" She already knew the answer.

He smiled and rubbed his thumb across her swollen mouth. "Why do you ask questions you already know the answers to, little dove?"

She had no reply for that and he winked at her before lying beside her and cupping her breast. He rubbed at her nipple, watching as it tightened into a hard, little bud and her pale skin began to flush. He cupped her other breast, the nipple had already stiffened, and a moan escaped her throat when he traced it with the tip of one finger.

"Turn onto your stomach, Abigail."

She tensed and shook her head no and he frowned at her. "Why not?"

"I don't want to, okay?" She gave him a shaky smile. "Please, Val."

She reached down and took his cock into her hand, rubbing back and forth as he inhaled sharply.

With her other hand she tried to urge him on top of her. "Like this again, okay?"

He pulled her hand away from his cock and shook his head. "No. Turn over, Abigail."

The desire was fading from her eyes and he could see a secret lurking deep within their depths. He scowled. He didn't want her keeping anything from him. The look of anger on his face made her tense, and he placed a gentle hand on the swell of her belly.

"I won't, Val. Don't ask me again. I'll fuck you but only on my terms. Do you understand?"

"I do," he murmured soothingly. He bent his head and kissed her until her body relaxed and she was making soft noises of pleasure. She clung to him, her soft hands stroking his broad back and her hips arching repeatedly against him.

He released her mouth and gave her an apologetic smile. "Forgive me, little dove."

She blinked. "Forgive you for what?"

He flipped her effortlessly onto her stomach, pinning her upper body down with one hand between her shoulder blades.

Her yell of shock and outrage was muffled into the blanket and she whipped her head to the left and glared at him. "Goddamn you, Val!"

He didn't answer. He couldn't answer. The words were sucked out of him by the horrific sight of her back.

"Who did this to you?" He choked out.

She refused to answer and instead kicked at him. He put one leg over both of hers almost absentmindedly. She was no match for his strength and she collapsed against the blanket, nearly spitting at him in fury.

"You had no right to do that, Val! I told you I didn't want – "

"Hush, Abigail." He was still looking at her back. "You belong to me now, and there will be no secrets between us."

She gaped at him. "I do not belong to you!"

"Yes, you do," he spoke absently as if the subject was closed to further discussion. He leaned over her and examined her back closely. The pale, soft skin of her upper back was marred with ugly rope-like scars. He dropped his eyes to her lower back and snarled in silent rage when he saw the raised scar in the shape of a cross on her skin. "Tell me who did this to you. Now, little dove."

She sighed. "My foster mother."

"What's a foster mother?"

She squirmed again. "Let me up first."

∾ ∾

Val continued to stare at Abigail's scars as she said, "Let me up first."

He released her but before she could flip over he had hauled her into a sitting position between his own spread legs. He bent her forward slightly and pushed her long hair to the side so he could continue to look at her back.

Everywhere he looked he found something else that made his rage grow. Her back was covered with hundreds of thin, pale lines of scars that were nearly hidden by the larger scars. There were small round marks that could only be burns. On the back of her left shoulder, nearly hidden beneath a particularly large scar, the word 'whore' was carved into her skin in neat, block letters.

"My parents died when I was a toddler. I had no other relatives so in my world they put you into what they call 'foster care.' Other people are paid to take care of you." Abigail said.

She cleared her throat and raised her knees, leaning away from him and resting her arms on her knees and her chin on her arms. "When I was seven I was put in a foster home with a woman and her husband. The husband was, well, he wasn't normal but he wasn't crazy. The woman was a complete lunatic. She was religious and made me spend hours on my knees praying and asking for forgiveness of my sins."

"What were your sins?"

She shrugged. "Anything and everything. Slamming the door was a sin, toothpaste in the sink was a sin, laughing too loudly was a sin. The rules changed every day."

"She said that God came to her every night and told her whether I was truly repentant of my sins for that day. If he told her I had prayed hard enough and he had forgiven me then I wasn't beaten. If not, she would whip me with a leather belt in the morning. Or sometimes she used piano wire."

She stared moodily at the side of the stall. "Just between you and me - if God did come to visit her every night, that guy is a real dick. I prayed for hours every night, begging for forgiveness, and I still got almost daily beatings."

"Was there no one to help you? No one that you could go to?"

"Diana said she would kill me if I told anyone. She told me God would strike me dead with lightning before I even had the chance to tell people what she was doing. I was only a child and scared to death. To this day, I hate thunder and lightning storms."

He reached out to trace the word carved into her skin and was not surprised to see his hand shaking with rage. "And this?"

She actually laughed a little. "Diana carved that into my skin when I was fourteen and she found a romance novel in my schoolbag."

"A romance novel?" Val looked at her doubtfully.

"It's a book about – about a man and a woman falling in love. Anyway, one of my few friends had tossed it in there as a joke. I hadn't even read the damn book. She took forever to carve it – nearly an entire day. She said she wanted my future husband to be able to read it clearly and know what he had married."

He gave another low snarl of anger and she jumped a little, turning her head to give him a cautious look. "Val? I – are you okay?" He knew that his eyes were glowing and his normally pale skin had a dark flush.

He forced himself to calm down and touched the cross on her back. "How did she do this?"

She gave him a startled look. "Does the – does the cross repel you?"

He surprised himself and her by laughing. "No, little dove. Vampire's being hurt or scared off by a cross is nothing but an old witch tale."

"But silver hurts – it can kill you," she whispered.

"Yes. Silver, a stake to the heart, sunlight and chopping its head off will kill a vampire."

He leaned forward and pressed his lips against the scar. "Tell me how she did this."

"She had a metal cross that hung over the front door. There was no real reason for this one - at least not that I could tell. I came home from school one day and she was in the kitchen heating up the cross in the oven. She made me strip off my shirt and bend over the table and then she very calmly took the cross out of the oven and pressed it against my back."

"I would kill her for what she has done," he said furiously.

"It was a long time ago," she replied. "For all I know she could already be dead."

"How did you escape?"

"I didn't. I lived there until I was eighteen and then they stopped paying her and she kicked me out. I could have run away, I guess. But I was too weak and afraid."

She sighed softly. "I'm always afraid."

"I can't believe you survived without going mad."

"I created a safe place," she said in a toneless little whisper. "When she started to – to hurt me, I went to my safe place and stayed there until she was done."

He frowned. "Where is your safe place?"

She shrugged. "I don't know. I close my eyes and concentrate and then I'm there. It's so pretty, Val. It has white flowers and the sun is always shining. The grass is soft and no one can find me there."

She sighed. "At least it used to be that way."

He turned her head toward him. Her eyes were soft and faraway and he stroked her cheek with his thumb. "What do you mean?"

She raised her gaze to his. "You found me. I was in my safe place and you came to me. We were naked and making love in the flowers. But then I realized that I really was going to go mad because I couldn't get away from you anymore. You had found me."

Tears were beginning to slide down her cheeks and he brushed them away. "I'm sorry, little dove."

She dropped her head onto her raised knees. "Can we stop talking about this now? I don't like to talk about it. And I'd like to go back to the house and get some sleep."

"Soon," he murmured.

He was lying. Abigail would sleep but not in the house. She would stay here with him, wrapped in his arms until dawn and only then would he send her away.

He bent his head and placed soft, wet kisses across the scars on her back. She stiffened and tried to pull away but he held her firmly as he continued to caress her back with his mouth.

"Val," she moaned and he turned her until she was straddling his lap. He stared down at her pale body and she flushed and tried to cover herself with her arms.

"Don't do that." He frowned and pulled her arms away. "I would see all of you."

She flushed even brighter. "You think I'm ugly."

"I don't," he insisted. "I'm sorry I told you that. It isn't true."

He grasped her chin and made her look at him. "I think you're beautiful, Abigail. The most beautiful woman I've ever seen. If I didn't, do you think I would be here with you now, about to make you mine again?"

She swallowed hard. "You're doing this only

because you want to feed from me."

"No." He brushed his lips against hers. "I could seduce and feed from you without taking your body. I want you, Abigail."

He took her hand and pressed it against his throbbing erection as he used his other hand to cup her breast, rubbing his thumb over her hard nipple.

"Do you see what you do to me? What I do to you? We were meant for each other."

She shook her head. "No. It's because you've bitten me. Once we've reached Karna I'll never see you again and my lust will fade."

He kissed her, his tongue probing between her lips and tracing her smooth teeth, before he sucked on her lower lip. "No, little dove. It is more than that. When we reach Karna, I will not abandon you. I will take care of you, provide for you, and in return you will pleasure me with your body."

"Val, I can't - "

He plucked at her nipple and she moaned under her breath.

"You belong to me, little dove. Let me take care of you."

કર્જ જ્જ

Abigail closed her eyes. It was pointless to resist Val. She needed someone to take care of her. She was weak and afraid, and she knew she wouldn't last long in this world without someone like Val to watch out for her.

He smiled at her wordless surrender and pulled her closer until his cock was brushing against her wet center. She moaned again and her fingers dug into the hard flesh of his shoulders when he lifted one heavy breast and ran his tongue over her nipple. He lifted her up to settle her down onto his cock and she had time to marvel at his strength before his cock was sliding into her. He pulled her even closer, urging her to wrap her legs around his waist.

They kissed hotly, their tongues sucking and sliding against each other's as she rolled her hips against him. He cupped her ass, his fingers digging into her flesh, and he lifted her up and down on his cock. She gasped his name as he placed his mouth on her shoulder. His fangs slipped into the small holes already there and he made a low moan as her blood flowed into his mouth.

She cried out and squeezed compulsively around him, her entire body shaking with her orgasm as he continued to thrust back and forth. He forced himself to stop drinking and licked his lips clean of her blood as he pushed in and out of her hot and soaking wet pussy.

He weaved his fingers through her long dark hair, yanking her head back so he could trail kisses down her smooth skin. He resisted the urge to bite her neck and growled into her ear. "Tighten around me, Abigail. Squeeze your tight pussy around my cock right now."

She moaned at his hotly-whispered command and clenched her muscles around him. He groaned at the added pressure on his cock and plunged into her twice more before coming violently inside of her.

She collapsed against his lap and he stroked her long hair before kissing her on the cheek. She was weak and limp, nearly asleep already, and he laid her on the blanket. She curled up on her side almost immediately, tucking one hand under her cheek, as he stretched out behind her. He spooned her, sliding his hand around her to cup one full breast.

"So tired," she whispered wearily.

"I know, little dove. Go to sleep." He kissed the back of her shoulder as she slipped into slumber.

Chapter Eight

"She's letting him feed from her. She must be," Neil murmured to Maria. It was two days later and he watched as Abigail laughed at something Bert said to her as she walked behind the wagon.

Maria nodded. "She is. She's been sneaking out each night to meet him."

"Why is she hiding it? We all understand why she is doing it."

"I do not know."

"She told me that in her world vampires were considered the undead. That they had no heartbeat and no soul and were evil."

"Aye. My husband said the same thing," Maria said solemnly.

"Perhaps that is why she feels the need to hide it from us. If she believes that Val is evil then she may be ashamed by her desire for him," Neil said hesitantly.

"Perhaps."

They watched as David joined her and smiled down at her. She smiled back and he took her hand.

She squeezed it briefly before dropping it and a small frown crossed David's face.

"He is in love with her," Maria sighed.

Neil grinned. "You think? She could do worse. David is a good man."

Maria frowned. "Is he? Sometimes I wonder."

"What do you mean?"

Maria shook her head. "Nothing. He's wasting his time anyway. She belongs to Val now."

Neil gave her a puzzled look. "Once we reach Karna and she is away from Val, her need will fade. Why shouldn't David have a chance with her then?"

Maria rolled her eyes. "For a smart guy you sure are dumb, Neil."

He flushed. "I've known Val for many years, Maria. He will never become infatuated with a human."

She laughed. "He already has. You can see it every time he looks at her. Did you not see the look on his face last night when David sat so close to her? He has been hiding his own need for her, probably because she has asked him to do so, but he won't be able to hide it much longer. Especially if David continues to touch her."

"What are you saying? That once we reach Karna he will set up house with her?"

Maria shrugged. "There are vampires who are doing that exact thing in Karna."

"Never with a human – they keep to their own kind. Besides, Val is – he's…" Neil trailed off.

"He's what, Neil? Val may be a vampire but it doesn't mean he is not capable of love."

"I know that. But I never thought that Val

would care about anything but himself. I mean, for a leech, he's kind enough, but he's been a vampire for over five hundred years. He's forgotten what it means to be human."

"I thought Val was your friend."

"He is. But it doesn't mean that I believe he's capable of loving anyone but himself, or that I have to approve of his plan to keep Abby as a pet." Neil's voice was growing louder and Maria glanced around worriedly.

"Neil, keep your voice down!" She muttered.

"Abby is a nice girl and she deserves someone like David, not Val," Neil said heatedly, although he lowered his voice.

"She's in love with Val," Maria said softly.

"Horse shit," Neil spat. "She's infatuated with him because he bit her, nothing more."

Maria held up her hands. "Okay, Neil. Calm down."

Neil, breathing heavily, stared furiously at her. "She is not in love with him, Maria."

"Tell me why you're so upset," Maria suddenly said.

"I'm not upset." Neil gave her a cautious look.

"Yes you are. And I want to know why. We have been friends for a few years now and I know hardly anything about you. You're friends with Val, hell you stick up for the vampires more than any other human I know, and I want to know why the thought of Abby being in love with Val is so upsetting to you."

Neil sighed harshly. "I was married once."

Maria stared at him in shock. "I had no idea."

"Her name was Atina. I loved her so much, Maria. We grew up in the same village and I think I fell in love with her when I was still a small boy. We married young. She was nineteen and I was twenty."

"What happened to her?" Maria asked.

"A pack of vampires overtook our village for a time. There were more of them back then, although their numbers were already starting to dwindle. They didn't stay long – a month maybe – but it was long enough. They fed from a bunch of us and Atina, she wasn't a strong woman. She was sweet and gentle and when the head vampire fed from her, she became obsessed with him."

He raked his hand through his short dark hair. "I tried to tell her that it would fade with time and that the vampire felt nothing for her. She didn't – couldn't – believe me. When the vampires eventually left she became withdrawn and depressed. Two weeks later she took her own life."

"Oh Neil." Maria squeezed his arm. "I'm so sorry. I'm surprised you don't hate them."

He shrugged. "I did. For years I couldn't stand their kind or how they treated the humans. But then Val saved my life and I realized that they're similar to us in that there are good ones and bad ones, you know?"

Maria grunted. "Val and Eone are the only good vampires I've met and it might be a stretch to call them good."

"Yeah," Neil agreed. "Anyway, as grateful as I am to Val for saving my life we need to keep Abigail away from him when we reach Karna. She deserves the chance to realize that what she feels for him is just because he's feeding from her."

"And if it isn't?" Maria asked.

"It is," Neil replied.

ॐ ॐ

"If he keeps touching you, I'll kill him."

Val's voice drifted out of the darkness and Abby raised her head from where it rested on his chest. She was listening to the steady beat of his heart and marveling between the differences in the mythical vampires of her world and the reality of vampires in this one.

"You're overreacting."

He sat up in the bed and ran a hand through his long hair. "No, I'm not."

"Yes, you are." She sat up beside him and tucked the covers around her naked body. "And keep your voice down please."

They had found lodging for the night in a house that was surprisingly large. Nearly everyone had claimed their own room and shortly after dinner Abby had retired to her room, using a headache as an excuse. She had found Val waiting for her in her room as she knew she would.

"He touches you constantly and he gives me this look like he has won you in a game of barnen." Val's hands were rolling into fists and she rubbed his back.

"David and I are friends, nothing more."

He gave her a wry look. "David wants between your legs, Abigail. Do not pretend otherwise."

She sighed. What Val was saying was true and

she had no idea how to deal with it. In her world, men weren't attracted to her. She had slept with exactly one person before Val, and it had only happened because both she and her best friend Carl were drunk. Her cheeks burned and her pulse increased at the memory of the next morning. Carl had woken up, taken one look at her, and skedaddled his ass out of her apartment as fast as he could. He had refused to take any of her calls after that, and she had mourned the loss of their friendship more than the loss of her virginity.

Darkness crossed Val's face and he pushed her onto her back on the bed. He covered her soft curves with his broad body and rested his hand on her hip. He threaded the fingers of his other hand through her dark hair and held it tightly.

"You're blushing and I can hear your pulse increasing." He leaned down and sniffed her pulse at the base of her neck.

He looked up at her and her breath caught in her throat at the look of anger in his eyes. "Have you let the boy between your thighs, little dove? Has he dared to touch what belongs to me?"

He reached between her thighs and cupped her possessively as his thumb parted her labia and found her clit. He stroked it roughly and brushed his mouth across her trembling lips.

"I would hear the truth from you, little dove. But I should warn you that if I find out you've let him kiss you, allowed him to put his fingers or his cock inside of you," he slid his finger into her tight pussy and grinned with satisfaction at her soft moan of submission, "I really will kill him - very slowly and very painfully."

"He hasn't done any of those things."

"But you want him to." His voice was dangerously soft.

She shook her head. "No, I don't."

He thumbed her clit in approval and she arched her hips against him.

"Then why do you blush? Why is your pulse thudding so heavily?" He murmured into her ear.

"I was remembering something from my past."

"What?" He rubbed her clit again and she moaned a little and dug her nails into his broad arm.

"Nothing I want to talk about."

He frowned. "There are to be no secrets between us. Remember, little dove? Tell me what the memory was."

She snorted angrily and pushed his arm away before sitting up. His gaze drifted down to her naked breasts and she smacked him on the chest before yanking up the sheet.

"That's bullshit, Val, and you know it. I don't know anything about you. Every time I've asked, you distract me."

He arched his eyebrows at her uncharacteristic anger and leaned back against the headboard. "Ask me anything you want, Abigail."

"When did you become a vampire?"

"I was turned five hundred and twenty-four years ago."

"How old were you when you died?"

He frowned. "I was thirty-five but I didn't die, Abigail. I was turned before I could die."

She nodded. "Sorry. In my world, vampires are

considered undead."

He laughed. "Right, Neil told me. We have no heartbeat and no soul. Our skin is cold as ice and we always kill the humans we feed from. Your world is very dreary, little dove."

"It isn't!" She pursed her lips. "Can you eat real food?"

He nodded and she cocked her head at him. "I've never seen you eat or drink anything but blood."

"Not true. You've watched me eat your sweet pussy." He grinned at the hot blush that rose in her cheeks and he reached out and traced her soft skin. "Your cream tastes nearly as good as your blood, little dove."

"Stop distracting me." She pushed his hand away and he took her hand and held it firmly.

"Some vampires eat quite a bit of food even though it provides no nutrition for us. But many of us find it difficult to abandon that which made us human."

"So, you'll die without blood?"

"Eventually. It would take months though. The humans have experimented on us in the past, and I believe the longest a vampire lived without blood was nine months."

She gave him a horrified look. "They experimented on vampires?"

"Yes." He didn't seem bothered by it.

"Why?"

"Two hundred years ago there were many more of us. We weren't particularly kind to the humans. I suppose they believe they were justified in their experimentation on us."

"Are there not as many of you now?" She asked curiously.

"No. There was a sickness among us about a hundred and twenty years ago. It killed many of my kind."

"A sickness? I thought you were immortal. What type of sickness could kill you?"

He shrugged carelessly but she thought she saw a hint of pain in his eyes. "I don't know."

"How did you survive it?"

"Some were immune. They did tests, tried to figure out what it was that made some vampires immune, but never discovered what it was. They did, however, realize that the blood of the immune helped heal those who were sick."

She paused and then decided to ask the question. "Did you lose anyone special to you?"

"No."

He was lying, she could see it in his eyes, but she let it go. "How many humans have you killed?"

"Many. But they were all trying to kill me," he said honestly. "Does that bother you?"

"A little."

"I would never hurt you, little dove." He squeezed her hand.

"I know. Why did you leave your own kind for the humans?"

"What memory were you thinking of earlier?" He countered.

She looked down at their clasped hands. "I was remembering the first guy I slept with."

"Were you in love with him?"

She shook her head as Violet flew in through the slightly-open bedroom window. She flew to Abby and landed on her shoulder, winding her cold body into Abby's hair before kissing her on the side of the neck.

Abby smiled. "I was starting to worry about you, Violet. Where have you been, little one?"

Violet yawned and shrugged before sitting cross-legged on Abigail's shoulder. She leaned against her throat and stuck her tongue out at Val.

"Watch it, bug. I hear pixie blood is very sweet tasting," he growled playfully.

Violet rolled her eyes as Abby squeezed his hand. "Don't say things like that to her."

"Tell me about him," he prompted.

"His name was Carl. He was my best friend. One night we both ended up drunk and we slept together. In the morning, when he woke up in my bed, he was horrified by what he had done. He left and refused to speak to me ever again."

"He was a fool."

She shrugged. "I don't blame him."

"Tell me about your other lovers." The thought of other men touching her filled him with a strange rage but he wanted to know everything there was about Abigail.

She blushed. "There weren't any others."

"What do you mean?"

Her blush brightened. "I mean that before you, Carl was the only man I'd slept with."

"Why?"

She gave him a strange look. "Why? Well, because look at me, Val. I'm ugly. Even if I wasn't fat, I'm too pale, my nose is too big and my hair is too frizzy. Men aren't attracted to me. I honestly have no idea why David is."

He stared at her and realized she believed what she was saying. His chest tightened painfully and he reached out and gripped her chin. "He's attracted to you for the same reasons that I am. You're gorgeous and sweet and way too kind-hearted for your own good."

"You want me because of my blood," she whispered. "Don't lie to me, Val."

He shifted closer to her and cupped her face. "Your blood is very appealing to me, little dove, but it is not just that. You have become," he hesitated, "important to me. It is not just your blood that calls to me but everything about you."

His eyes skimmed over her face before he stared steadily at her. "Do you believe me?"

She looked down at the bed covers. "I don't know."

"Then let me show you once more," he whispered. He kissed her soft mouth and then stared at Violet still wrapped in Abby's hair.

"Go on, bug."

She huffed at him before kissing Abby's throat again. As she untangled herself from the long dark strands, Abby reached up and stroked her back with one finger.

"Good night, little one."

Violet flew to the basket on the far dresser. Abigail had fashioned a bed for her in the basket and without looking at either of them, the pixie burrowed deep under the layers of fabric until she was completely hidden within them.

Val pulled down the quilt, baring Abigail's breasts to his hot gaze. He dipped his head and trailed a blazing hot path down her chest before cupping one breast and capturing her nipple between his lips. He licked and sucked on it until it hardened in his mouth and Abigail's hands were tangled in his long hair.

"Lie back, little dove," he whispered.

Her body throbbing with need, Abby lay back against the pillows as Val kissed his way down her body. He dipped his tongue into her navel, circled it with his tongue and then blew on her damp skin.

She moaned and put her arm over her mouth to dampen the noise as he shifted until he was stretched out between her legs.

"So sweet," he murmured before he nibbled on her dripping pussy. She ground her hips against his face as his tongue probed between her lips to find her swollen clit. He licked it with rough strokes until her ample hips were rising from the bed and her hand was clutching frantically at the back of his head.

"Come for me, little dove," he whispered before sucking her clit into his mouth.

With a muffled shout, she did what he asked, her hand leaving the back of his head to clench around the quilt. As her orgasm rushed through her, she felt the sharp sting of his fangs on her inner thigh. He suckled on her skin, drinking her blood as her climax roared through her. Only when she had collapsed weakly on the bed, her arm falling away from her mouth and her breasts heaving as she struggled to pull in air, did he stop drinking.

He positioned himself over her and entered her dripping pussy with one smooth stroke. She arched beneath him, taking him deep inside of her, and he groaned his approval when her pussy muscles rippled around his thick cock.

"Open your eyes, little dove," he demanded.

Her eyelids fluttered open and he smiled down at her. "That's right, my love. Look at me and watch what you do to me."

He thrust in and out of her. Her pussy gripped him greedily, sucking at his cock and refusing to let go when he tried to retreat. He moaned with pleasure and she slapped her hand over his mouth. He licked the palm of her hand, making her shudder against him, before beginning to plunge in and out. The smooth tightness of her pussy, the way it clung wetly to him, brought him quickly to the edge and with a loud groan he thrust hard and climaxed inside of her.

Panting, he rolled off of her and collapsed on his back beside her. After a few minutes he turned on his side. When she didn't turn so that he could spoon her, he reached out and lifted her, moving her into the position he wanted her in.

Although she had seen Val's strength multiple times, Abigail was still surprised whenever he moved her two hundred-pound plus body like she weighed no more than a feather. As he threw his leg over her hip and his hand cupped her breast, she tried to squirm away.

Val growled under his breath and pulled her even closer. "Where are you going?"

"I'm not going anywhere," she grumbled. "You know I need space to sleep."

He laughed and kissed the back of her neck. "I'm leaving soon to go on watch with Eone. Indulge me until then."

She sighed and relaxed against him. "Will you come back before you go to your daysleep?"

He nodded. "Yes, little dove. I'll see you in a few hours. Go to sleep, Abigail."

Chapter Nine

"Abby will you take a walk with me?"

She smiled at David before glancing quickly at the wagon. After a long day of traveling, they were unable to find shelter and were once more camping in the open. It was almost twilight, Val would be awake soon and looking for her.

"Right now, David?"

He nodded. "Please? I wish to speak with you in private."

She pressed her lips together and then nodded. "Just a quick walk, okay? I need to help Maria with dinner."

He smiled and tried to take her hand as they walked deeper into the woods. She folded her arms across her torso, ignoring the disappointed look he gave her.

"You've done very well in denying the leech, Abby. I want you to know how proud I am of you."

"Thank you," she muttered. She looked down at the ground. She hated lying and was horrible at it. If she looked David in the eye, he would see the truth in her face.

"I know it hasn't been easy, not with that asshole leech staring at you all the time but –"

"Don't call him an asshole, David," she interrupted. "He's saved all of our lives."

He snorted angrily. "He almost killed you by drinking too much of your blood after you offered to save his miserable life. And trust me, if push came to shove, he'd abandon our asses."

"Did he abandon you at the village? Neil said if it hadn't been for him and Eone, none of you would have survived. Remember?"

He stopped suddenly and took her arms. "Why do you defend him, Abby?"

He tilted her chin up and stared into her face. "Why are you so quick to…"

He trailed off, his ruddy face paling at the look on her face. "Oh my God."

"David, I - "

"You've been letting him feed from you," he whispered. "Haven't you?"

"That's none of your business, David."

He surprised her by grabbing her hair and yanking her head back. She gave a soft cry of pain as he searched her throat for the tell-tale marks.

"Where is he biting you?" He snarled.

"Let me go!" She punched at him and he grabbed her wrists with one hand and ground the thin bones together.

She cried out with pain again as he tore at the neckline of her shirt. He sucked in his breath at the lightly-bruised bite marks on the soft meat of her shoulder and cursed vehemently before shoving her away.

She stumbled and nearly fell before rubbing her wrists and glaring at him. "You're a dickhead, David."

"Yeah, well you're nothing but a dirty leech whore. I should have known you - "

She slapped him as hard as she could across the face and his head rocked back. He cupped his cheek, staring in disbelief at her. She turned to run as he lunged for her, her scream cut off by his hard hand clamping across her mouth.

"I thought you were different, Abigail," he whispered into her ear. He turned her around and stared into her frightened eyes as he tightened his arm around her waist. "I was falling in love with you. Did you know that? I was so amazed by your ability to resist him, so impressed by your strength, that I actually thought I was in love with you."

She made a muffled sound against his palm and tried to pull away.

"Shh, don't do that. I should have known better than to think you were strong. The ones that come from your world are always so weak. They never survive long in our world."

He lowered her to the ground and straddled her before putting his thick hands around her throat. "You lied to me, Abigail. I could forgive you for submitting to the leech but not for lying to me."

"You don't have to do this, David," she begged as tears leaked from her eyes.

"I do, Abby," he whispered. "It's for your own good. It's better for you to be dead then to be with him."

She looked into his eyes and realized with sudden, terrifying clarity that he was insane. Something small and purple skated past the edge of her vision and she prayed that Violet would bring the others before it was too late. She dug her nails into his thick, hairy wrists and tried to heave him off of her. He growled with pain but settled himself more firmly on top of her.

He began to squeeze her throat and before her air supply was cut off, she choked out, "He'll kill you."

"He'll never know," he crooned.

❧ ❧

Val looked around the campsite and frowned. Abigail was nowhere to be seen and there was a bad feeling growing in his stomach.

"Neil, have you seen Abby?"

The big man shook his head. "She was right here. I'm not sure where she went."

"Where is David?" Val suddenly asked harshly.

"He's unloading the wagon. At least, I thought he was," Neil replied.

He shouted across the clearing to Landon. "Landon, have you seen David?"

The younger man shrugged and continued to build up the campfire.

There was a sharp tug on Val's hair and he turned to see Violet, her purple skin flushed and her eyes wide and frantic, staring at him.

"Where is she?" There was an unfamiliar sensation in his stomach and after a second he recognized it as fear. "Where is she, bug?"

Violet made a choking motion with her hands and pointed into the woods. He snarled and, as Violet darted into his hair and wrapped her small fists around it, he raced into the trees.

కొ ఇ

Abby pulled weakly at David's hands. Black roses were blooming in her vision and her feet drummed helplessly on the ground as his hands squeezed tightly around her throat. She mouthed Val's name as tears leaked down her cheeks.

There was a loud snarling and David was torn away from her. Choking and gasping she rolled to her side, grabbing at her throat as she fought to tear air into her throbbing lungs. Vaguely, she was aware of Violet hovering over her as David screamed pitifully.

"You dare to touch her?" Val roared. His hand around David's throat, he shook him like a rag doll. The big man screamed again as Val threw him to the ground.

"Please!" He begged as Val dragged him to his knees. Snarling and spitting, his fangs extended to an almost impossible length, Val bent towards him.

"Val no!" Abigail tried to scream and produced nothing but a hoarse whisper.

He turned to her and she shrank back at the sheer rage in his gaze.

"Wait," she whispered and then watched in horror as Val bent his mouth to David's throat and ripped it open.

David made a gurgling noise and clutched at his throat as blood gushed down his chest and onto the ground. He collapsed forward as Val wiped the blood from his mouth and walked towards Abby. She stared wordlessly at him, her hand rubbing at her throat, and he knelt down. She flinched when he reached for her and a look of pain flickered across his face.

"I will never hurt you, little dove. I promise you." He cupped the back of her head and drew her toward him. He rested his forehead against hers as Violet hovered anxiously over them.

"Do not be afraid of me, Abigail. Please," he whispered pleadingly.

With a soft cry she threw her arms around him and he hugged her hard. "You're safe, little dove."

He helped her to her feet and tilted her head up to look at her throat. Bruises were starting on her throat and he made a soft sound of distress. She tried to peer around him at David's body and he stopped her.

"No, little dove. Do not look at him."

He kissed her mouth and she returned his kiss before burying her face in his throat.

"Come, we need to get back to - "

A sudden shrill scream made them both jump and he turned toward the camp as more screams rang out.

"Stay here!" He demanded and took off in a blur.

Abigail hesitated only briefly before chasing after him. Panting, dragging air in through her swollen throat, she stumbled through the trees.

Her breath hissed out of her lungs when she reached the campsite. Ten vampires were tearing through the people in the campsite. She watched in horror as a short, fat vampire grabbed Erin by the hair and yanked her head back. He buried his face in her throat and she screamed as he bit into her skin. As he drank, he tore her throat wide with one long and dirty fingernail. Her blood sprayed out and he lapped at it like a dog, grinning and sucking at her neck as she sank to the ground.

Neil, his face grim, swung his sword in a wide arc, beheading the vampire that was about to sink her teeth into Maria's neck. She exploded into ash as Neil helped Maria to her feet.

"Go!" He roared. "Under the wagon – now!"

Maria scurried towards the compartment under the wagon as Eone and Val, hissing and snarling, attacked the vampires. She watched wide-eyed as they quickly dispatched the vampires, their swords flashing in the gloom.

Violet clung to Abigail's neck, hiding her face in her hair, as Neil and Val worked together to kill the last vampire. They had him cornered against the wagon and he dropped to his knees and held his hands up in surrender.

"Please no! I will leave! I'm sorry! I will not -"

His words died off in a gurgling little moan as Val thrust his sword into his chest. He stared up at Val, his eyes wide with shock and pain, before he exploded into ash.

Neil, panting harshly, looked around the campsite. "Oh my God," he whispered. Dead people lay scattered across the campsite. Only he and Maria had survived the carnage.

Violet released her grip on Abby's hair and fluttered a few feet away. She hovered, looking with horror at the dead people on the ground.

Val, his silver eyes glowing and his pale skin flushed with colour, frowned when he saw Abby standing next to a tree.

"Little dove, I told you to stay - "

His mouth dropped open in wordless horror when a vampire appeared out of thin air next to Abigail. He wrapped his arms around her body, hissed at Val, and disappeared with her in a flash of light.

Neil watched as Val dropped his sword and ran to where she had been. The vampire fell to his knees, a low keening starting in his chest. The keening quickly became a scream as he opened his mouth and wailed his pain into the night air.

Eone approached him gingerly. "Val, I am sorry. She is gone."

He turned on her and snarled, baring his fangs at her. "I will find her! Do you hear me, Eone? I will find her!"

"It's too late, Val," Eone replied. "She is probably already dead."

He screamed again and Neil flinched when Maria grabbed his arm. "Neil, what do we do?"

"I don't know," Neil replied quietly.

He watched as Val staggered to his feet and stared at them with haunted eyes. The vampire paid no attention when Violet darted forward and buried herself in his long hair, clinging grimly to the long strands.

"I will find her," he whispered hoarsely before disappearing into the trees.

About the Author

Ramona Gray is a Canadian romance author. She currently lives in Alberta with her awesome husband and her mutant Chihuahua. She's addicted to home improvement shows, good coffee, and reading and writing about the steamier moments in life.

If you would like more information about Ramona, please visit her at:

www.ramonagray.ca

Books by Ramona Gray

Individual Books

The Escort
Saving Jax
The Assistant
One Night
Sharing Del

Other World Series

The Vampire's Kiss (Book One)
The Vampire's Love (Book Two)
The Shifter's Mate (Book Three)
Rescued By The Wolf (Book Four)
Claiming Quinn (Book Five)
Choosing Rose (Book Six)

Undeniable Series

Undeniably His
Undeniably Hers

Printed in Great Britain
by Amazon

55271967R00068